disturbingly
normal

---

novel
J.D. Lenzen

illustrations
R. Black

authorHOUSE®

AuthorHouse™
1663 Liberty Drive
Bloomington, IN 47403
www.authorhouse.com
Phone: 1-800-839-8640

First published by AuthorHouse 4/22/2010

ISBN: 978-1-4520-0281-1 (e)
ISBN: 978-1-4520-0279-8 (sc)

Library of Congress Control Number: 2010904681

Printed in the United States of America
Bloomington, Indiana

This book is printed on acid-free paper.

Other Books by J.D. Lenzen

Soft Candy (2007)

For Kristen B. Kakos

contents

disturbingly
normal

the barista

Ben Morris knows more than he wants to about Jonathan Normal. They met a year and a half ago at the Black Rose coffee shop in the Upper Haight District of San Francisco. Ben was a nightshift barista and Jonathan was one of his regular customers.

Jonathan had messy, short brown hair, pouty full lips and calm brown eyes that transcended his twenty-five years of life. No matter how bright the day, he wore an untucked black dress shirt, black jeans, and black boots. This shadowy attire, along with a persistent *please don't bother me* look on his face, pushed the eyes of most away, but not the eyes of Ben.

Jonathan usually arrived a few hours before the coffee shop closed. He'd order the same drink, a mint-chocolate mocha, and he'd sit at one of the two tables that provided a view of the frenzied hum of the Haight. On the nights Ben was busy with customers Jonathan would gaze out the window until closing and then leave without a word. But on nights when customers were scarce, Jonathan would break from his usual brooding silence and talk to Ben for hours—typically well past closing.

More truthfully, their talks amounted to stories Jonathan told and Ben listened to while he straightened up, wiped down tables, or cleaned the espresso machine. Nevertheless, Ben enjoyed his time with Jonathan and appreciated the company he provided.

Of all the stories Jonathan told, Ben's favorite was shared with him shortly after he and Jonathan first met. Customers were sparse that night and Ben was considering closing early when Jonathan, one of three customers he'd served all night, looked up from his coffee and started to speak.

"Did you hear about the man in upstate New York who found the skeleton of a woolly mammoth in his backyard pond?"

Ben finished stacking the dishes he was holding, looked over at Jonathan, and smiled. "No, I didn't."

Jonathan took a sip of his coffee. "Scientists think it got stuck in the pond's mud some fourteen thousand years ago."

Ben circled out from behind the service counter, walked over to a chair near Jonathan, and sat down. "Where did you hear that?"

"I listen to NPR while I work," Jonathan said as he took another sip of his coffee. "The story came on during one of the news breaks."

Partly because he was curious and partly because he wanted to encourage more conversation, Ben asked Jonathan where he worked.

Jonathan looked down at his cup. "I don't like talking about work. I thought I mentioned that."

He had mentioned that. But, at the time, Ben had thought it was on account he'd had an especially bad day at work, not because he was establishing a conversational guideline. Nevertheless, he apologized for forgetting and awkwardly attempted to redirect the conversation by asking Jonathan if *he'd* ever been stuck in the mud.

A faint smile grew on Jonathan's face. "Yeah, I've been stuck in the mud."

Ben smiled. "Tell me about it."

Jonathan slipped his left hand into his left front pant pocket, pulled out a pocket watch, and looked at the face. "It's kind of a long story."

Ben scanned the coffee shop, "Everyone and their mother's decided to boycott the consumption of coffee tonight. I've got the time."

Jonathan leaned forward in his seat. "One summer, when I was a kid, my best friend Joe and I decided to walk across a storm channel near my house—we were about eight at the time. It was a dry summer that year, and the water in the channel, which usually stretched the width of a football field, was reduced to the width of a four-lane street. So, we thought we'd get our shoes wet, at worst, no big deal. We were way wrong.

"Each step Joe and I took toward the opposite end of the channel sank us deeper into mud. Joe was afraid he'd get stuck, so he turned back. But I pressed on, rationalizing I was already a mess, so I might as well go for it.

Jonathan took a breath. "Before I knew it, the channel mud was up to my calves, and then my knees. From there I just started sinking, until it was finally up to my waist, and I was officially stuck.

"By this time, Joe was standing safely on the bank, and although he wanted to help me out, we both knew there wasn't much he could do. So, I told him to run to my house and get my dad.

"As I watched Joe scurry up and over the bank of the channel, I figured he'd return with my dad, I'd get pulled out of the mud, and that would be that. But while my dad was rummaging through our garage looking for rope, he told my mom what'd happened. My mom has a tendency to overreact. So when Melissa Fischer, our next-door neighbor's daughter, overheard my mom's wailing fears, she ran and called her best friend, Jessica. Melissa told Jessica something to the effect that I was 'moments away from suffocating in the mud of the channel.' Jessica called her friends, who all called their friends, and so on and so forth. Until, forty-five minutes from the time Joe ran to get my dad, fifty-two bystanders, three police cars, a fire engine, an ambulance, and a local news crew were all scattered along the bank of the storm channel waiting to see if the 'mud boy' was gonna be all right."

"That's crazy!" Ben said.

"That's not even the worst of it… Thinking he'd pull me out, my dad took the rope he'd brought back from our house, held on to one end, and tossed the other out to me. Then he hollered out instructions for a bowline and told me to tie the rope around my waist. When I was done tying, my dad started pulling—I didn't budge an inch. So he got a bunch of guys from the crowd to help him out. This time,

I not only didn't budge, the rope cinched so tight I could barely breathe.

"My dad thinks this is on account I accidentally tied a slipknot instead of a bowline, but I'm pretty sure I tied it right.

"Anyway, a few moments later, while I was adjusting the rope around my waist, I heard someone call out that they had a solution. It was the voice of a policeman, and silence swept across the crowd as he spoke. 'If the boy could get his bowline tied correctly,' the policeman said indignantly, 'I could tie the other end of the rope to the bumper of my car and we could inch him out.'

"When I heard mumbled agreement from the crowd I nearly wet my shorts. Thankfully, my dad had more sense. 'Inch my boy out with your patrol car?' he questioned. 'Are you nuts? He nearly got cut in half when we just had men pulling on him!' Then, thank God, Patrick Moore spoke up.

"Mr. Moore was the owner of Moore's Lumber Yard and a neighborhood friend of my dad. His thought, tile the mud like you would a floor. 'If we lined up the tiles properly,' Mr. Moore said, 'a person could get close enough to dig out some of that mud. After that, someone could pull him straight up and out.'

"It was a brilliant idea, and it didn't involve pain, suffering, or accidental dismemberment—plusses for me.

"Thirty minutes later, a fireman was standing over me, shoveling out the mud that was pressing against my body. Once he'd created a gap, the fireman bent down and cupped his hands underneath my armpits. Then he counted to three and began to pull.

"By this time, I'd been stuck in the mud for a little over two hours, during which time I'd only been able to move my arms, shoulders, and head. So, it felt good to see freedom in sight. But just as I was starting to smile, I felt my shoes and socks peel off my feet. When I mentioned this fact to the fireman, he paused and resentfully asked, 'Do you want to get out of this mud or not?' I told him I did, and he heaved one more time. With a *harrumph*, I was freed, but completely naked from the waist down—my shoes, socks, underwear, and shorts, all sacrificed to the mud beneath me.

"As soon as the fireman let go of me, I tried to stretch my t-shirt down to cover myself. But, I couldn't get it to stretch much farther than my waist. So, in a fit of pure desperation, I started to run.

"I ran over the plywood tiles, maneuvered around the crowds of people, jetted up and over the channel and down the streets that led to my house. I ran so fast and so hard that by the time I reached my driveway, I dropped from exhaustion. My parents arrived home a short time later, and were thankfully sympathetic to my embarrassment. Unfortunately, the news crew that covered the incident wasn't.

"Although they assured me and my parents they wouldn't, and in fact didn't, air their tape of my uncovered bottom, they did make repeated mention of it and had an on-air laugh at my expense."

That was one of Jonathan's earlier stories. The others that came before, and most of the ones that came after, were similar only in that they all revolved around the memory of an experience he'd once had. Still, not all his stories were light-hearted ones. Over time, he'd reflect upon, and occasionally share, darker moments from his life. The most unnerving of which was shared with Ben the last time the two spoke.

It was a Friday night, and the Black Rose had been closed for nearly an hour. Ben had just finished mopping up and was about to lock up and leave when he heard someone pounding on the front window.

A closer looked revealed it was Jonathan. He looked worn out and tired, and the sockets of his eyes were red, like he'd been crying and then wiped them dry with his knuckles.

"Can we talk?" Jonathan called out from the other side of the window.

"Why?" Ben asked.

Jonathan reached out a hand and pressed his palm against the glass. "Because you listen…"

Ben was genuinely concerned by Jonathan's distressed look, but he'd also just ended a ten-hour shift and hadn't eaten a thing all day. So he asked Jonathan if he'd be up for talking over food.

"No problem," Jonathan replied. "I'm kind of hungry myself."

Ben took a second look at Jonathan. There was intensity in his eyes he hadn't seen before, a fire that surprised him. "Meet me at Sparky's."

Sparky's was one of a handful of 24-hour diners in the city. Subsequently, it was something of a refuge for club-goers, tweakers, insomniacs, and night-shifters looking for an after-hour meal.

Although Jonathan had left for Sparky's before Ben had, Ben was parked and standing at the entrance before him. The reason for this was simple; Jonathan drove a car and Ben drove a scooter. Finding a parking space for a car in San Francisco isn't impossible, but it takes time. Ben, on the other hand, could find a parking spot for his Vespa PX just about anywhere.

As soon as Ben saw Jonathan walking toward him, the hostess called out, "Ben, table for two!"

"Good timing," Ben said as Jonathan walked up. "Our table's ready."

Jonathan didn't look pleased.

Ben walked through the front door, following behind the hostess.

Jonathan slid up beside him and sighed. "I really need to talk to you."

Ben turned and looked at Jonathan. "We'll talk."

"Alone, away from here…"

The hostess pointed at a table and Ben sat down. "I thought you said you were hungry?"

Jonathan remained standing. "I lied."

Irritated by Jonathan's fickle disposition, and a bit testy on account of his hunger, Ben snapped back, "Well, I didn't! So if you want to talk to me, you're gonna have to do it while you watch me eat."

Jonathan sighed and sat down across from Ben. "All right."

A few moments later, the waiter arrived. He was wearing bright red glitter lipstick, blue eye shadow, a pink tutu, and a circa-1979 Shaun Cassidy and Parker Stevenson *Hardy Boys Mysteries* t-shirt. Ben and Jonathan looked at each other and smiled.

After taking Ben's order for a bowl of mashed potatoes with gravy, chili-cheese fries, two slices of toasted sourdough bread, and a Coke, the waiter asked Jonathan what he'd like.

Before answering, Jonathan locked eyes with Ben and asked, "Are you actually planning to eat all that?"

"Of course," Ben replied indignantly. "Why?"

Jonathan sat back. "Forget I asked." He handed the waiter his menu. "I'll have a Coke."

Once the waiter was gone, Ben decided to capitalize on Jonathan's and his shared smile by asking him if he'd ever seen a waiter as decked out as theirs was.

Jonathan ignored Ben's question. "Can we talk now?"

Ben huffed. "Sure."

"Something happened today. Something horrible, that I don't remember, but I'm pretty sure I did."

"Something happened where?"

Jonathan sighed. "At work."

Ben leaned forward in his seat. "Correct me if I'm wrong, but I thought you don't like to talk about work?"

"Forget about that," Jonathan said. "There's something I need to get off my chest. Something I'm hoping you can help me understand."

By this point, Ben didn't care why Jonathan was backpedaling on the subject of his job. He was more curious what had gotten him so worked up. So he sat back and crossed his arms. "I'm listening."

Jonathan leaned forward and whispered, "I'm a mortuary driver."

Ben turned an ear toward Jonathan. "A what?"

Jonathan waited for a customer to pass by the table and then continued. "I pick up human remains for a mortuary in Oakland."

"Okay."

Jonathan scowled. "I'm not a freak!"

"Relax," Ben said. "I don't think you're a freak. What mortuary do you work for?"

"Christian-Collins. At least I did, until today."

"You were fired?"

"Yeah."

"Did they have a reason?"

Jonathan picked the salt shaker up off the table and started toying with it. "They had a reason."

"What was it?"

Jonathan set the shaker down and wiped his hands over his face. "This afternoon, I picked up a man named Robert Ray Lewis. He died of cancer at Kaiser Hospital in Oakland. A doctor supervised his death, so all his paperwork was in order." Jonathan clasped his hands in front of him and looked down at the table. "All I had to do was drive him four blocks. Four stupid blocks... But I slipped into a blur."

"A what?"

Jonathan's eyes started to tear up. "I blacked out. Things got hazy, I don't know..."

Sympathetic to Jonathan's tears, Ben reached out and gripped one of his hands.

Jonathan looked up and over Ben's shoulder and then pulled his hand away.

Ben looked back and saw their waiter.

"Two Cokes," the waiter said as he set down their drinks.

"Thanks," Ben said as the waiter walked off.

Jonathan took a breath and continued. "When I came to again, I was in the Berkeley hills, near Tilden Park. The hearse was parked on the side of the road, and I was standing outside the driver side door."

"Let me get this straight. You blacked out and woke up standing?"

"Yeah."

"That's odd."

Jonathan looked at Ben flatly, "It gets worse."

Ben swallowed. "Go on."

"I tried to open the door, but it was locked. So I reached into my pockets to see if I had the keys." Jonathan paused and took a slow, deep breath. "I found a credit card receipt from Big 5 Sporting Goods in my right pocket. The time on the receipt was two-twelve p.m., an hour after the pickup, and the signature on it was mine."

"What was the receipt for?"

"An aluminum baseball bat."

"And you don't remember buying it?"

Jonathan cleared his throat. "No."

Ben was starting to get uncomfortable. "I'm sure there's a legitimate reason for all this. One you can look into and get taken care of." He thought for a moment. "Maybe you have walking narcolepsy or something?"

Jonathan grimaced. "There's more."

Ben wiped a hand over his mouth.

"When I circled around the back of the hearse, I found the back door open and Robert Ray Lewis's body sprawled out on the ground."

Ben tensed.

"His body was bludgeoned and there was a blood-stained aluminum baseball bat lying next to him on the ground."

Ben studied Jonathan's face. "Are you fucking with me?"

"No."

"Then why are you telling me this?"

Jonathan pursed his lips. "I have no one else to talk to."

Ben was unsettled by Jonathan's confession and pretty much wanted to get the hell out of Sparky's and away from the conversation. But at the same time, he didn't want to agitate him further. So he suggested that he get his food to go, so they could continue their conversation outside. From there, Ben figured, he'd politely excuse himself.

"I feel bad," Jonathan said. "I didn't mean to spoil your night."

"Really, it's cool," Ben replied nervously. "Just let me settle the bill and get my things bagged up. I'll walk you to your car. We can talk more on the way. Okay?"

Jonathan sighed. "Okay... But, if you don't mind, I'm gonna wait outside for you."

Ben mustered up the most convincing smile he could. "No problem."

After paying the bill and leaving a tip for the waiter, Ben walked outside. A few steps from the door, Jonathan was hugging an attractive black girl good-bye. She had long, pencil-thick braids that flowed down over her back, high cheekbones, and dark catlike eyes. And she seemed to know Jonathan well. After the girl walked away, Ben walked up to Jonathan. "A friend?" he asked.

"Yeah," Jonathan replied as he reached into his back pocket and pulled out his wallet. "What do I owe you?"

"Don't worry about it," Ben said. "You only had a Coke. I covered it."

"Thanks."

"What's her name?"

"Tonya," Jonathan said in a soft voice.

"Who is she?"

"A friend... She's on her way home from a party."

"She's beautiful," Ben commented.

Jonathan looked off in the direction Tonya walked. She looked back and he waved at her. "In more ways than you could ever imagine."

The sincerity in Jonathan's voice intrigued Ben, stalling his planned exit long enough for Jonathan to say, "My car's parked a block down the street. If you're still up for talking?"

"I am," Ben replied, surprised by his response.

As Ben walked beside Jonathan, his nerves started to get the best of him—until, underneath a street lamp, less than a block from Sparky's, he stopped. "This is as far as I go," he said.

"Something wrong?"

"I like you, Jonathan. Really, I do. But what you just told me was pretty unsettling." Ben pursed his lips. "See, I don't really know you. You're one of my customers, and I like you and all, but—"

"I could be some kind of freak," Jonathan interjected.

Ben stepped back. "I'm sorry, but what am I supposed to think?"

Jonathan looked down, ran his fingers through his hair, and started to cry. "I don't know!"

Ben took a breath. "Were you high?"

Jonathan looked up. "Was I what?"

"High," Ben repeated.

"No, I wasn't high!" Jonathan snapped back. He shook his head and started walking away.

A surge of pity rose within Ben. "Okay, then," he called out. "Have you ever done this before?"

Just outside the illumination of the street lamp, Jonathan stopped walking and turned around. His face was streaked with tears. "No!"

"Then why this unconscious urge to beat the body of this man named—" Ben paused to think.

Jonathan sniffled. "Robert Ray Lewis. And, I don't know!"

Ben walked up to Jonathan. "You said you slipped into a blur."

Jonathan wiped his eyes with the palms of his hands. "So?"

"Do you remember thinking or feeling anything?"

Jonathan looked down, reached up with one hand, and started scratching the front of his neck. "Hate," he said. "I remember feeling hate."

Ben felt a lump in his throat. "Was Robert Ray Lewis black?"

Jonathan stopped scratching, looked up and locked eyes with Ben. "Yeah, he was black, why?"

"Was it a racial thing?"

"That's what Mr. Pestana asked."

"Who's Mr. Pestana?"

"My boss."

Ben was stunned. "Your boss knows about this?"

"Why do you think I was fired?"

"Is he pressing charges?"

Jonathan rolled his eyes. "He won't press charges."

"Are you sure about that?"

"The press would kill business. Besides, Mr. Pestana told me he wouldn't."

"When did he tell you that?"

"At the mortuary...after I put the body back into the hearse, I found the keys dangling off the back lock. So I drove to the mortuary and told Mr. Pestana everything I just told you."

"What'd he say?"

"He said he'd repair the body, make it look like nothing happened, and that he wouldn't press charges."

"That's it?"

Jonathan paused as if in thought. "He also said I was fired and that if I told anyone what I did, he'd have me arrested."

"But you told me."

"I had to tell someone!"

Ben flinched.

Jonathan grimaced. "What do you think I should do?"

14

"You should thank your lucky stars you're not going to jail!" Ben snapped. "That's what you should do."

"I'm serious."

"So am I!"

Jonathan turned away from Ben and walked to his car.

Another surge of pity rose within Ben. "When was the last time you took a vacation?"

"Never," Jonathan said, yanking open the driver side door.

"Well, maybe it's time you took one," Ben said. "Get away for a while. The rest might help you make sense of what happened."

Jonathan looked back at Ben. "I've always wanted to take a road trip up the coast, visit old friends, maybe see Canada."

Ben's face softened. "Then I say do it."

For a moment it looked as if Jonathan was going to say something else. Instead, he got into the car and started it up. He rolled down the window and called out, "Thanks."

"For what?" Ben asked.

"For listening."

Ben smiled. "Take care of yourself Jonathan."

"I will," Jonathan replied, and then sped off down the street, out of sight and out of Ben's life.

the ex-girlfriend

Every November 2, at 7:30 p.m., an All Souls' Day procession passed by Tonya Baker's apartment. For years, her traditional response to this event was to curse under her breath, go about her business, and wait impatiently for the procession to pass. But last year, she got up, situated herself, and went outside to take a look.

When she emerged onto the street she saw a crowd of people all watching what looked like a parade. But unlike a traditional parade, this one had no floats, no flashy cars, and no smiling prom queens. Instead, groups of people whose bodies were painted to look like skeletons wobbled down the street like drunken puppets. They tossed out candy, held up massive papier-mâché figures of deathly brides and grooms, blew on bent trumpets, and beat on punctured drums. It was a cacophony of motion, color, and sound, and Tonya watched on in giddy amazement—wondering why she'd waited so long to view such a fantastic event.

"Hey, you, in the pink hoodie and leather pants!"

Although she was pretty sure she was the only girl in the crowd wearing said attire, Tonya took a quick look around just to make sure. As she surveyed the clothes of the people around her, she heard, "Up here!"

Tonya looked up and saw a handsome young man sitting atop a bus stop enclosure. He was wearing an untucked black collared shirt, black jeans, and a black pair of boots.

The young man patted the space beside him. "There's room for one more, if you'd like to get a better view."

Tonya liked the vantage point and the look of the company being offered. "Do you know where I might find the hand of a gentleman to help me up?"

"As it just so happens," the young man said as he leaned over and reached out a hand, "I do."

Moments later, Tonya was sitting comfortably with a queen's view of the procession. Appreciative, she turned, smiled, and reached out her hand for a shake. "Tonya Baker."

The young man reached out and shook Tonya's hand. "Jonathan Normal."

"Thanks for helping me up."

"No problem."

Tonya looked down at the crowd of people below. "Why'd you offer me a seat and not one of them?"

"You looked like you'd appreciate a better view," Jonathan said. "And, you're wearing leather."

Tonya looked at Jonathan, her smile growing. "Ahh. You like leather."

Jonathan laughed nervously. "A lot, yeah."

"Good."

"Why good?"

"'Cuz leather's what I mostly wear."

Jonathan grinned. "Ever been to a Day of the Dead procession before?"

Tonya looked over the procession. "I thought today was All Souls' Day."

"According to the Roman Catholic Church, it is. But to the people of Mexico, today's El Dia De Los Muertos, the Day of the Dead."

"I should come clean," Tonya said as she settled back onto her elbows. "Aside from the fact that I'm enjoying myself, I don't know much about any of this. It's all new to me."

"I could fill you in on the details."

Tonya smiled. "I'd like that."

"According to Mexican folklore, today's the day when the dead return to earth and enjoy the pleasures of the living. So people, mostly in rural Mexico, visit the cemetery where their loved ones are buried and decorate their graves with marigolds and candles. They bring toys for the dead children, bottles of tequila for the dead adults, and extravagant foods and candies for everyone else." Jonathan tucked a leg under his seat. "Did you see the sugar skulls and chocolate coffins tossed into the crowd?"

Tonya rose off her elbows and sat up. "I saw 'em."

"Those are ceremonial offerings to the dead. Once those offerings are made, the spirits of the dead eat, dance, and celebrate. Their family members join in the celebration, and together, the dead and the living picnic, laugh, and party!"

Tonya looked at the procession. "So, *it's a dead man's party...*"

"*Who could ask for more?*"

Tonya turned and smiled at Jonathan. "So why is everyone here so upbeat about death?"

"Not everyone views death as the end of life. The Aztecs, for instance, viewed it as the continuation of life. So instead of fearing it, they embraced it. To them, life was a dream and death the awakening."

Tonya looked back at the procession. "What do you think?"

"About death?"

"Yeah."

"I think it marks the first day of a soul's migration to another place."

"A migration to where?"

Jonathan shrugged his shoulders. "I don't know for sure. I suppose I'll find out when I get there."

As Jonathan talked, Tonya found herself smiling a lot. So, when a soft rain started to fall and the tail end of the procession passed, she was disappointed that soon, she and he would likely part ways.

"It's starting to rain," Jonathan commented.

"Yes it is," Tonya replied as she tucked her braids back and flipped her hoodie over her head.

Jonathan held out an open hand. "I love the rain."

Tonya shook her head. "You like leather and rain?

Jonathan smiled. "Uh-huh."

"I can't think of two things that go together less."

Jonathan's gaze settled on Tonya's eyes. "I'm unconventional."

Tonya stuffed her hands into the pockets of her hoodie and looked up into the sky. "What's so good about rain, aside from obvious things like nourishing our bodies and keeping plants alive?"

"When it rains," Jonathan said in a soft voice, "streets that are usually crowded clear, parks empty and—"

"People get wet," Tonya interjected.

"Some people look better wet."

"Really?" Tonya questioned with a smile.

Jonathan looked away sheepishly. "I'm just saying..."

Tonya shook her head, still smiling. "Right."

Jonathan climbed down off the bus stop enclosure. "Come, walk with me in the rain," he said.

"You're not serious?"

"I'm totally serious," Jonathan said. He settled onto the sidewalk and reached out a hand toward Tonya.

Tonya shook her head and smiled. There were so many reasons why her taking a walk in the rain was a bad idea. The fact that she was wearing leather was the first. There was also her hair, which didn't respond well to uncontrolled moisture. Then there was her makeup. "I'm gonna fall apart," she said. "My hair's gonna poof out and my makeup's gonna run."

"If you don't mind, I don't either," Jonathan said, still holding his hand out.

"You don't even have a jacket!"

Jonathan smiled. "I'll be fine."

Tonya reached out and took Jonathan's hand. "Okay... I'll go."

A few minutes later, Tonya and Jonathan were walking side by side down a rain-soaked sidewalk.

"Where are you from?" Tonya asked.

"East Bay," Jonathan said.

"Where about?"

"Niles."

Tonya paused in thought. "Never heard of it."

"It's a district of Fremont. Charlie Chaplin shot a bunch of films there."

"Ah," Tonya said knowingly. "Still live there?"

"Not since I was seventeen. I moved to Arcata after high school, did a year at Humboldt State, and then moved back to the Bay Area. I've lived here in the city ever since."

"If you don't mind me asking, how old are you?"

"I don't mind. I'm twenty-four."

"Do you have sisters or brothers?"

"I'm an only child."

"Are you close to your parents?"

"Am I close to my parents?" Jonathan repeated. "I suppose so, but not on account I want to be."

"What do you mean?"

"I've got this theory: reality divided by expectations equals happiness."

Tonya thought for a moment and then smiled. "Okay..."

"Well... My dad's vision of family life developed through 1950s television shows like *The Adventures of Ozzie & Harriet* and *Father Knows Best*. So his expectations were a dutiful wife and compliant, agreeable children. What he got was my mom, a neurotic woman with obsessive compulsions, and me, a depressed kid who wanted little if anything to do with either one of them."

"What kind of obsessive compulsions?"

"She cleaned incessantly, everyday, seven days a week—drove my Dad and me nuts. The worst was when she cleaned the bathroom."

"Why the bathroom?"

"Because once she was finished, you couldn't use it for at least two hours."

"Why not?"

"It's a trip, but from my mom's perspective, using something that was just cleaned messed with her head. It sent her into a tirade. 'You're not gonna use the bathroom? I just cleaned it, for Christ's sake!'"

"Jeez."

"Seriously, it was crazy."

"I'm so sorry."

"I'm totally over it," Jonathan said matter-of-factly and then hesitated for a moment. "Okay, maybe not *totally*, but mostly."

"Are your parents still together?"

"It's hard to believe, but yeah."

Tonya took a breath. "I grew up in Arkansas."

"What part?"

"Newport. You know it?"

"I don't."

"It's in Jackson County, about 80 miles northeast of Little Rock. It's a small-ass town, and I'm glad I left. Only wish I coulda took my mom and my sister with me."

"You have a sister?"

"Yeah." Tonya smiled. "Her name's Lynette. She's nineteen. Still lives at home with my mom."

"And your dad?"

Tonya looked away. "Sore subject, next question."

"Okay," Jonathan said without missing a beat. "What brought you to San Francisco?"

Tonya looked back at Jonathan. "A boyfriend. He moved here for a sales job at Oracle, and I came along with him. Two months later, Oracle laid him off. He moved back to Arkansas. I stayed."

"Was that difficult for you?"

"Was what difficult?"

"Leaving your boyfriend."

"My god, no! Our relationship was already on the rocks as it was. His job falling through like it did was a blessing for us both." Tonya took a couple of steps in silence. "What do you do for a living?"

"What do you think I do?" Jonathan replied coyly.

Tonya looked Jonathan over. "You dress like a moody philosopher."

"That's impressive," Jonathan said playfully. "Most people aren't familiar with the moody philosopher dress code. Truth is, I used to be a moody philosopher, but I abandoned the profession after discovering how many Marxists it took to change a light bulb."

Tonya smiled awkwardly. "I don't get it."

"It's a dumb joke... What do you do for cash?"

Tonya raised an eyebrow. "I break things for a living."

Jonathan smiled. "So you're a game tester."

"How'd you know?"

"Game testers always say that."

Tonya smirked. "I suppose I could say I sit in front of a computer for hours on end, performing scripted tasks in search of programming glitches. But that doesn't sound as sexy."

"You have a point there."

The rain stopped and the night sky started to clear. Jonathan's shirt was damp, but not excessively wet. Still, as Tonya walked beside him, glancing over now and then with a smile, something told her he wouldn't have cared if he was soaked to the bone. "How are you holding up?"

"Fine... You?"

"I'm good." Tonya glanced down at her wristwatch—it was almost nine o'clock.

"How's my time looking?" Jonathan asked.

"Your time?" Tonya questioned.

"How much more time do I have before you have to go?"

"Where are we heading?"

"Down Mission Street, we're coming up on 16th."

Tonya playfully socked Jonathan in his arm. "Duh… Do you have a destination in mind?"

"How about Upper Haight?"

"For what?"

"Coffee?"

"That's a stupid long distance for coffee."

Jonathan sighed. "I suppose."

Tonya stopped walking. "What are you doing tomorrow night around six?"

Jonathan turned and faced Tonya. "Nothing, why?"

"'Cuz I'm about to head back home. But I want to see you again. So tomorrow night, you're gonna take me to dinner."

"I am?" Jonathan asked, pointing to himself.

Tonya smiled. "You are."

After scrambling for a pen and paper, Tonya and Jonathan exchanged numbers and then waved goodbye. The following night, Jonathan took Tonya to dinner, afterward Tonya took Jonathan back to her apartment.

Over the course of the next three months, Jonathan and Tonya dated regularly. It was during this time that Tonya learned that aside from the occasional bout of animated storytelling, Jonathan was pretty much a depressed, chronically sullen guy. Still, their relationship was manageable. The sex was good, and she enjoyed spending time with him. Things changed the day she found out what he did for a living.

The discovery took place while they were walking back to Tonya's apartment. Tonya had gone grocery shopping and Jonathan had gone with her. As they walked down the street, Jonathan holding Tonya's bag of groceries and Tonya walking beside him, she looked over at him and asked, "What do you do for a living?"

"That's funny," he commented.

"Why?" Tonya asked, puzzled by Jonathan's response.

"You've never asked me that before."

Tonya paused. "Actually I did, the night we met. But you skirted the subject so I dropped it."

Jonathan took a breath.

"Well?"

"I don't know..."

"You don't know what you do for a living?"

"I don't know if I should tell you."

"Why not?"

Jonathan paused. "People have a hard time dealing with my job."

"If you don't want to tell me," Tonya commented abruptly, "forget I asked."

"It's not that," Jonathan said and then continued. "I'm a mortuary driver."

Tonya was stunned. "You're a mortician?"

"Not a mortician!" Jonathan snapped back. "A mortuary driver. I pick up bodies and transport them to a mortuary."

Tonya paused. "That's some job."

"Does it bother you?"

"No," Tonya said as she looked away from Jonathan. "How long have you been a mortuary driver?"

"Two years." Jonathan set Tonya's bag of groceries down on the sidewalk. "Are you okay?"

"I'm fine... Just give me a moment."

"A moment for what?"

Tonya looked back at Jonathan. "To absorb."

"Absorb what?"

"Your job!"

"What's there to absorb? I'm a taxi driver for dead people. So what?"

Tonya locked eyes with Jonathan. "Do you touch the bodies?"

"With gloves on, yeah… When I transfer them to the hearse… Why?"

"'Cuz we've been intimate."

Jonathan reached out for one of Tonya's hands. "I wear gloves," he repeated.

Tonya pulled away.

"What the fuck?" Jonathan questioned angrily.

"Please!" Tonya insisted. "I need a moment."

Jonathan kicked Tonya's bag of groceries, oranges spilled out. "Take as long as you want!" he said and stormed off.

Tonya dropped to her knees and started gathering her groceries. "That was totally unnecessary!"

Jonathan didn't respond.

"Jonathan," Tonya called out. "Jonathan!"

For months, neither Tonya nor Jonathan attempted to contact one another. Tonya's lack of effort was on account she'd grown tired of their relationship, the street side meltdown making for an easy out. Naively she'd thought Jonathan's lack of effort was for similar reasons, but she was wrong. A fact she discovered at a barbecue her friend Brandon was hosting.

Brandon was a distinguished looking man with long hair and a goatee. More often than not, he wore a black tailcoat, black tights, and black military jump boots, a look that his wife termed "gothic ringmaster". He and Tonya met at a fetish party he produced called *Slick*. She was attending the party with friends when Brandon approached her, introduced himself, and asked her for a unique favor.

Autumn Adamme, a designer of custom corsets and owner of the corset boutique Dark Garden, was putting on a fashion show that night. But one of her corset models didn't show. Brandon asked Tonya if she'd fill in. Tonya said yes, modeled, and had an amazing night. Brandon and she had been friends ever since.

Brandon and his wife, Kristen, lived in an Edwardian flat nestled in the center of the Castro District. Together they decorated their home with a mismatched array of *A Nightmare Before Christmas* memorabilia, dried flowers, rubber bats, and other oddities. Still, the showpiece of their space was Einstein, a 12-year-old parrot, who lived in a cage adjacent to the front door.

On the day of the barbecue, as Tonya walked into Brandon and Kristen's flat, she noticed Einstein's pupils dilate and contract in rapid succession—something she'd seen a few times before. "Why do Einstein's pupils flex like that?" she asked Brandon as she set her coat down on a couch next to Einstein's cage.

"It's called eye-blazing," Brandon replied. "It just means he's excited."

Tonya grimaced. "Is he gonna be okay?"

Brandon stood beside Tonya, hooked his arm around hers and smiled. "He'll be fine. May I escort you to the back deck?"

Tonya curtsied. "If that's where the barbecue is, that's where I want to be."

"It is indeed," Brandon replied as he led Tonya to the back of the flat, out a door that opened onto a deck and right into Jonathan.

"Jonathan," Tonya said nervously.

"Tonya," Jonathan replied.

Brandon released Tonya's arm, took a moment to survey the situation, and then raised a finger into the air. "I think I just heard the doorbell."

Tonya shook her head as Brandon walked off, and then greeted Jonathan with a smile. "So how you been?"

"Fine," Jonathan replied. "And you?"

"Good," Tonya said.

There was an awkward silence.

"I didn't know you knew Brandon."

"Who?" Jonathan asked.

"Brandon—the guy you just saw."

"Right… He introduced himself as Random."

"Random's his nickname."

"I just met him today."

"How'd you end up here?"

"I'm picking up my roommate."

"I didn't know you had one."

Jonathan paused. "He just moved in."

"You two heading somewhere?"

"Nowhere special… Just back home."

Someone inside the house called Jonathan's name.

Tonya looked toward the sound and saw a tall guy with short, spiky hair tip a finger toward Jonathan. "I'll be out front!"

"Thanks," Jonathan called back.

"Well," Tonya said. "I suppose you don't want to keep your roommate waiting."

"He can wait," Jonathan said as he locked eyes with Tonya and took a breath. "Look, I'm sorry."

Tonya smirked. "What are you sorry about?"

"I completely overreacted last time we saw each other, and I had no reason to leave you like I did. I thought about calling you and apologizing sooner, but I didn't. So, again, I'm sorry."

"It wasn't just you," Tonya replied. She reached out and took Jonathan's hand. "I could have just as easily called you, but I didn't."

Jonathan looked down at Tonya's hand holding his and smiled. "I'll tell you what," he said.

"What's that?"

"I'll call you."

"You will?"

"Yeah."

"I'd like that."

The next night, Tonya and Jonathan talked on the phone for nearly two hours, learning more about each other than they'd ever known before. They talked about their dreams, their fears, and their frustrations. They talked so freely and so unabashedly that, as their conversation came to a close, Tonya seriously wondered if she'd feel uncomfortable around Jonathan for having revealed so much. She was thankful no such feelings materialized, and over the course of the weeks that followed, she and Jonathan continued to grow closer to one another. So close that when she saw Jonathan looking disheveled an anxious during a chance Friday night encounter, she was deeply concerned.

Tonya was walking down Church Street, on her way home from a friend's birthday party, when she stumbled upon Jonathan sitting on the curb in front of Sparky's.

"Tonya!" Jonathan exclaimed as he stood up from the curb. "What are you doing here?"

"I'm on my way home from a party. Are you waiting for a table?"

"Finishing up… A friend's inside paying our bill."

Tonya looked Jonathan over. His clothes were wrinkled and dirty, and he seemed restless. "Are you okay?"

"Of course I'm okay," he replied with blatantly feigned assuredness.

"Come on, Jonathan," Tonya said. "You know I know you better than that."

Jonathan sighed. "All right… I'm not okay. But I don't have time to go into it right now."

"Why? What happened?"

Jonathan glanced into Sparky's. "Really… I don't have time."

Tonya was worried by Jonathan's appearance and disposition. But, she could tell he wanted her to leave, so out of respect for his wishes, she obliged him. "Call me," she said as she reached out and hugged Jonathan good-bye.

"I will," Jonathan whispered into her ear as he let go.

After reaching the end of the block, Tonya glanced back and saw Jonathan talking to his friend.

Jonathan waved at her.

Tonya waved back, and then continued home.

Later that same weekend, while Tonya was settling into bed, her phone rang. It was early Sunday morning.

"Did I wake you?" Jonathan asked in a strained voice.

"No," Tonya replied. "What's up?"

"I'm leaving town for a while, and I wanted you to know."

"Is everything okay?"

"Everything's fine. I just need some time to myself."

"Where are you going?"

Jonathan cleared his throat. "On a road trip up the coast. I have friends in Arcata and Ashland, so I'll probably drop by and visit 'em as I pass through."

"Are you sure your car'll be okay?"

"Of course…"

"Jonathan, your radiator leaks like a sieve."

"I poured sealer into it last week. It isn't leaking anymore."

Tonya sighed. "Have it looked at before you leave. Please, for me."

"I don't have time. I've already packed my things. I'm heading out tonight."

"It's twelve-thirty… Get some sleep. Leave in the morning."

"I'll be fine," Jonathan insisted. "Besides, I haven't been able to sleep since Thursday."

"You haven't slept for two days?"

"It doesn't matter," Jonathan sighed.

"It matters Jonathan!"

Jonathan paused. "All right… I'll sleep tonight and leave in the morning."

"You promise?"

"I promise."

"Call me when you wake up."

"I will," Jonathan said. "Talk to you then."

As soon as Tonya set down the phone she started to doubt Jonathan would do what he said he would. So after an hour of wakeful worry, she got dressed, drove down to his apartment, and checked to see if his car was still parked out front—it wasn't.

Frustrated, Tonya pulled into a parking space where she had a clear sight of Jonathan's front door. There, she sat and thought about what to do next.

A few moments later she noticed a rectangular piece of paper taped to Jonathan's apartment window. She got out, walked up to the paper, saw that it was an envelope and pulled it off the glass. It was addressed to her. Inside was a note that read:

> *Dear Tonya,*
>
> *If I know you as well as you know me, you're standing outside my apartment reading this note, pissed off that I left.*
>
> *Life is unsettling for me right now, and the thought of spending time away from the city is the only thing that feels good. So, for now, I'm on the road, spending time away. When things settle down, I'll return.*
>
> *I wish I could tell you more, but I can't.*
>
> *Jonathan*

the
catalyst

the catalyst

Daniel Park was a fidgety man. So, rather than remain alone, stifled and understimulated in his Mill Valley apartment, he drove out to attend a free outdoor electronic dance party called the Reunion.

Held at Webster Lake Park in Novato, California, the Reunion was scheduled to begin at two o'clock, Sunday afternoon, and end shortly after sunset. Regretfully, Daniel didn't know this and showed up to the party at noon. At that hour, aside from the setup crew for the event, the park was essentially empty.

After asking the event coordinators if they needed any help setting up and being told they had it covered, Daniel decided to bide time with a hike into the hills above the lake.

On his way toward a trailhead pointed out to him by a park ranger, he noticed a vintage Mercedes-Benz and stopped to take a closer look.

Daniel had been a fan of rally cars his whole life, so he couldn't help himself from sizing up the car. It was a 1965 220S, with a gray body and red interior. The model had a renowned sporting heritage, winning first, second, and third place in the 1960 Monte Carlo Rally. Advanced for its time, it was the benchmark for all 1960s car manufacturers. Although Daniel knew it wasn't exceptionally rare, the car's stylish radiator grille and fintail back end drew him in.

As he peered into the backseat window of the car, he saw a young man sprawled out inside. His eyes were closed and he appeared to be sleeping restlessly. He was mumbling something aloud. Curious what the young man was saying, Daniel stepped closer and accidentally bumped his forehead on the car's window.

The man's eyes opened. "What the fuck!" he belted out as he scrambled back and smacked open the car door behind him. He spilled out onto the parking lot pavement.

"I'm so sorry," Daniel said apologetically. "I didn't mean to startle you."

The man got up off the ground, took a breath, and looked around.

"Are you okay?"

"I'm fine... Where am I?"

Daniel circled around the car. "Webster Lake Park in Novato."

"Novato!" the man exclaimed as he dusted himself off. "Jesus, I hardly got anywhere."

"Are you *sure* you're okay?"

"I'm fine... Why were you looking into my car?"

"I was admiring it."

The man gave Daniel a crooked look. "Come on. It's a piece of shit."

"I like rally cars. Your model was one of the best."

The man huffed.

"Are you here for the Reunion?"

"The what?"

"The Reunion," Daniel repeated as he pointed off toward a crew that was pulling equipment out the back of a moving truck. "It's a dance party. Starts in a couple of hours... All are welcome, if you want to attend."

"Thanks, but I'm just passing through."

"Where are you heading?"

"Up the coast," the man said as he reached into a pocket and pulled out a watch. "I pulled over for a short nap." He sighed. "So much for that idea..."

"You're on a schedule?"

"Not really... Just hoping to be further than Novato by now."

Daniel looked down at his wristwatch—it was 12:35 p.m. "Well, I'm heading out for a hike. My apologies for waking you up."

"No problem," the man said as he leaned into the back seat of his car. "Take care."

Daniel started walking off. Once he reached the trailhead he looked back toward the Mercedes-Benz and was surprised to see the man looking back at him.

"Sorry if I sounded grumpy," he said from a distance. "You woke me out of a bad dream."

"No worries... Enjoy your trip."

The man trotted up to Daniel. "How long do you think your hike'll last?"

"I don't know… An hour, maybe two. Why?"

The man reached up and rubbed the back of his neck. "I was wondering if I could go with you."

"You want to go hiking with me?"

"If that's okay?" the man replied sheepishly.

"Sure," Daniel said as he reached out his hand for a shake. "Name's Daniel Park."

The man gripped Daniel's hand and smiled back. "Jonathan Normal."

Daniel and Jonathan walked side by side along a trail that wrapped around the edge of a small pond. Then they traversed a creek, wove around a patch of willows, and passed under a stretch of California bays.

As the two entered a grassland area, Jonathan stopped in front of a valley oak tree. He reached out, felt its thick, ridged bark, and smiled. "How old do you think this tree is?" he asked.

Daniel shrugged his shoulders. "It's hard to say. They can live as long as six hundred years—I know that."

"Six hundred years," Jonathan said dreamily. "That's a lot of living." He looked at Daniel. "Wouldn't it be cool if trees could remember the past?"

Daniel looked at Jonathan intently. "If a tree grows, it remembers."

Jonathan paused. "What do you mean?"

"Every inch of growth on a tree is a stored memory of its life. From its days as a sapling on forward, a memory of every season, every trauma, and every time of plenty is stored within its wood." Daniel looked at the oak. "This oak is the living summation of every experience it's ever had."

Jonathan looked back at the oak and smiled. "I've never thought of a tree like that."

"How about yourself?"

"What about myself?"

"Have you ever thought of yourself like that?"

"Why would I?"

"Because it's true for us as well," Daniel replied as he started walking further down the trail.

Jonathan looked at the oak a few moments longer and then jogged to catch up with Daniel.

Daniel turned up a narrow path that ascended out of the grassland area and up through a cluster of buckeye trees. At the top of the rise, he sat down on a shaded bench with an elevated view of Webster Lake.

Jonathan sat down beside him. "I was thinking about what you said back at the oak," he said.

"What part?" Daniel questioned.

"The part about us being the summation of our life experiences."

"What about it?"

Jonathan took a breath. "What if someone does something really bad, something shameful or repulsive? Is that act forever a part of who they are?"

"You're asking my opinion?"

"Yeah."

"Yes. It will forever be a part of who they are."

Jonathan's shoulders sank. "So if a person does something horrible, they're a horrible person?"

"Sort of… Everything we do is an expression of who we are. But at the same time, our lives aren't set in stone. New bricks are laid every day."

Jonathan looked at Daniel. "You lost me."

Daniel stood up, walked forward a couple of steps, turned around, and faced Jonathan. "Consider a river."

Jonathan smiled. "All right, I'm considering."

"If you take a bucket of water from a river and study that bucket every day for weeks on end, would you understand the river?"

Jonathan paused as if in thought. "No."

"Why not?"

"Because a bucket of water isn't a river."

Daniel tapped the tip of his nose and winked. "Exactly!"

Jonathan chuckled. "I'm still lost."

Daniel sat back down next to Jonathan. "A river's a process. It's not a bucket of water. Likewise, you, I, and everyone else are processes—ever changing, ever dynamic. So, just as you can't study a bucket of water and say you understand a river, you can't review a single life moment and consider it the sum total of who you are."

Jonathan took a deep breath and stared off toward Webster Lake.

After a couple of minutes passed, Daniel stood up, stepped toward the lake, and stretched his arms out above his head. "Ready to move on?" he asked as he looked back at Jonathan.

Jonathan smiled. "Yeah."

Daniel and Jonathan continued following the trail they were on, past the shaded bench and down a long switchback trail bordered by hazelnuts, tan oaks, and buckeyes. At the base of the trail was a meadow circled by clusters of thimbleberry bushes.

Daniel walked up to one of the bushes, snapped a thimbleberry off its stalk, and popped it into his mouth. "Pick one," he said as he chewed. "They're delicious."

"I'm good," Jonathan replied as he stood beside Daniel, smiling and watching him eat.

"Suit yourself," Daniel said as he took hold of another thimbleberry.

"You're quite the philosopher."

Daniel finished chewing. "You think so?"

"Yeah!" Jonathan replied, apparently surprised by Daniel's response.

"I prefer to consider myself a catalyst."

Jonathan stuffed his hands into his pant pockets. "Why a catalyst?"

"Catalysts promote reactions, but don't themselves enter into them. I like the metaphor."

"I get that..." Jonathan said. "Mind if I ask you a question?"

"Not at all."

"You seem like a really cool guy, and I'm really happy I asked to come along on this hike."

Daniel smiled "Right..."

"But, at the same time," Jonathan continued. "I've got a lot on my mind."

"I sensed that."

Jonathan cleared his throat. "You did?"

"Yes," Daniel replied calmly. "It's very clear to me you have a lot on your mind."

"What else do you see?"

"In you?" Daniel questioned.

"Yeah."

Daniel took a breath. "I see someone who's conflicted and isn't fully comfortable with himself."

Jonathan sighed. "I feel like I'm struggling between the person I am and the person I want to be, and it sucks."

Daniel looked at Jonathan intently. "I'm not sure if this is gonna connect, but there's only one *you*. So everything you do and everything you are is perfect."

Jonathan huffed. "I'm hardly perfect."

"But that's the thing, you are." Daniel shot a finger gun at Jonathan. "Name one person who can out Jonathan Normal you... Someone who's exactly you, but better."

A smile slowly grew on Jonathan's face. "All right, okay. I get your point. But how do I know *perfect me* is on the right track?"

Daniel smiled. "Everything you do is 'on the right track.' The challenge is not wronging yourself every step of the way." Daniel took a breath. "Acceptance of your perfection leads to ownership of who you are, and ownership leads to choice—life's greatest gift."

Jonathan wiped his hands over his face. "I wish it was that simple."

"It is that simple."

Jonathan dropped his gaze.

"You're looking for direction?"

Jonathan looked up at Daniel. "I am."

"Back at your car, you said you'd just awoken from a dream."

"Yeah, so?"

"Do you remember it?"

Jonathan sighed. "Bits and pieces..."

"Would you be up for sharing?"

"Sure," Jonathan said. He gazed off toward the middle of the meadow. "I was in a room. There was a large window to my left and a cracked open door to my right. I was planning to do something...but I can't remember what." He looked at Daniel. "I heard someone call out my name. Then, I took a deep breath, closed my eyes and started to float."

"You started to fly?" Daniel asked.

Jonathan reached up and scratched his neck absently. "I stayed where I was and the house disappeared around me. From there on out, I was standing in the sky, feeling frightened and alone"—he looked down at his right palm—"holding purple lilacs in my hand."

"Lilacs."

"Yeah, they just appeared in my hand."

"Lilacs are a symbol of renewal and rebirth."

Jonathan huffed dismissively.

"Seriously," Daniel insisted. "What's your relationship to lilacs?"

"I don't have one."

"Recognizing lilacs suggests you know what they look like, correct?"

"Yeah, so?"

"So when did you first come to recognize lilacs?"

"When I was a kid, they grew wild along a creek near my house."

"Were these lilacs in bloom all year round?"

"No. They bloomed in the spring."

"So if someone blindfolded you, picked you up, and dropped you somewhere in time, blooming lilacs would be a good indication, wherever you stood, that it was spring, am I right?"

"I suppose so, yeah."

"And spring is a time of renewal and rebirth."

Jonathan stood in silence with a stunned look on his face.

Daniel rested a hand on Jonathan's shoulder. "I'm only pointing out that dreams mean things. And if direction is what you're looking for, you might want to pay attention to them." Daniel started walking toward the switchback trail. "Dreams are voices from within," he called back to Jonathan.

Jonathan remained in the in the meadow, silent, and thoughtful.

By the time Daniel made it back to the shaded bench, it was 2:35. Jonathan arrived at the bench a few minutes later.

Daniel looked off toward Webster Lake. The rhythmic thump of electronic music filled the air and hundreds of people were settled upon and moving about an obtuse triangular field of grass that arced alongside the northern stretch of the lake. "Looks like the party started."

Jonathan walked up and stood beside Daniel. "Jesus, where'd they all come from?"

"The Reunion is popular," Daniel commented as he reached into his back pocket and pulled out a clear, thumb-sized Ziploc baggie. He opened the baggie, pulled out one of two tiny square tabs, and causally set it onto his tongue.

"What's that?" Jonathan asked.

Daniel smiled. "Acid."

Jonathan pointed at Daniel's Ziploc baggie. "Mind if I take a look?"

Daniel handed the baggie over. "Not at all."

Jonathan held up the baggie and looked at the tab inside.

"It has a lavender bear on it," Daniel commented.

"I can see that," Jonathan said.

"If you want it, it's yours."

Jonathan lowered the baggie and looked off toward Webster Lake.

"You'd come on in about an hour," Daniel said, "and peak about three hours after that." He looked down at his wristwatch—it was 2:40 p.m. "If you stick it out 'til sunset, you should be able to drive out in relatively good shape."

Without looking away from his view of Webster Lake, Jonathan opened the baggie, pulled out the tab of acid and placed it onto his tongue. "I'm in," he said.

Daniel smiled. "Welcome!"

Upon their return to parking lot, Daniel and Jonathan emerged into a flurry of human activity. People were carrying blankets, coolers, and food toward the grass area they'd seen from above, and the sound of electronic music mixed with the sounds of conversation and laughter.

"Well," Jonathan said softly under his breath, "there's a first time for everything."

"Never been to an outdoor dance party before?"

Jonathan turned and looked at Daniel. "I've never done acid before."

Daniel's face shifted to a look of concern.

"Is that a problem?" Jonathan asked nervously.

Noticing the hesitation in Jonathan's voice, Daniel quickly perked up and smiled. "No problem at all. You'll have a blast."

Jonathan looked as if he was going to say something, but then stopped short of speaking as a girl walked up.

She had costume-quality butterfly wings on her shoulders. Her face was painted with purple and blue swirls, and she was holding a blue wand with silver strips of Mylar dangling from its tip.

"Carla!" Daniel exclaimed as he stepped in for a hug.

Carla smiled a giddy smile and opened her arms wide. "How have you been?" she asked as she wrapped her arms around Daniel.

Daniel let go of Carla and stepped back. "You know me, *always merry and bright.*"

Carla laughed.

Daniel placed a hand on Jonathan's back and looked earnestly at Carla. "I want you to meet a new friend of mine. His name's Jonathan Normal."

Carla smiled and shook her wand at Jonathan. "Hey there, Mr. Normal. I'm Carla. Nice to meet you."

Jonathan took a breath. "You too."

"Just so you know," Daniel said as he leaned in toward Carla, "Jonathan and I dropped acid about a half hour ago."

Carla batted her eyelashes. "Do you have any for me?"

Daniel grimaced. "I don't."

Carla playfully hit Daniel with her wand.

Daniel flinched. "I had no idea you were gonna be here."

"You could have called and asked if I was going."

"I don't do phones," Daniel commented. "You know that."

Carla rolled her eyes. "Whatever."

Jonathan looked away uncomfortably and sighed.

"You boys are welcome to join me on my blanket, if you'd like?"

Daniel looked at Jonathan. "You up for that?"

Jonathan shrugged. "Sure."

A few minutes later, Daniel, Jonathan, and Carla were all sitting together on a blanket stretched out amid a mosaic of blankets facing a dance area.

Carla leaned in toward Jonathan and pointed her wand toward the DJ. "That's Spesh. Daniel knew him when he was still called Special K."

Jonathan nodded. "Cool."

Carla sat back and smiled. "You dance there?"

Jonathan looked perplexed. "Dance where?"

"Qoöl!" Carla exclaimed.

Jonathan looked at Daniel. "You're friend's a trip."

Daniel smiled. "Qoöl's the name of a happy hour Spesh spins at in the city."

Jonathan looked away and sighed.

"Are you feeling something?" Daniel asked.

"Yeah," Jonathan replied in a flat voice.

Daniel leaned in. "What's it like?"

Jonathan flashed a faint smile. "Boredom."

Daniel sat back and smiled. "I'm not feeling anything either."

"Nothing?" Jonathan asked.

"Nada," Daniel said as he shook his head. He looked at his watch— it was 3:55 p.m. "We should've come on by now. But then again…"

"'Then again' what?" Jonathan asked.

"Responses vary," Daniel continued.

Carla crossed her arms and pouted. "I wish I could score some acid."

Daniel looked off over Carla's shoulder and then slowly stood.

"See someone you know?" Carla asked.

Daniel looked down at Carla and smiled. "Stand up."

Carla stood up. "What?"

Daniel pointed. "See that blond guy sitting next to that lanky dude with the black hair?"

Carla looked off in the direction Daniel was pointing. "Yeah."

Daniel dropped his hand back to his side. "The blond guy's name is Paul. Ask him if he can spare some lavender bears."

Carla looked at Daniel and smiled. "Are lavender bears what I think they are?"

Daniel smiled. "They are."

"Why don't you just come with me?"

"Because I've got to pee."

"I do too," Jonathan said as he stood up.

Carla started walking toward Paul, then stopped, spun around and looked back. "Daniel!"

"Yeah?"

"You're the best!"

As Carla spun back around, Daniel and Jonathan started toward the parking lot, where the porta-potties were. After Daniel finished peeing, he waited for Jonathan.

"Feeling anything now?" Daniel asked as Jonathan walked up to him.

"Nothing."

Daniel looked at his watch—it was 4:15 p.m. "I'm starting to think we got bunk tabs. Sometimes blotter sheets don't pan out evenly, and their edges are left untreated. Sorry about that."

"It's not a problem," Jonathan said. "Getting high sounded like a good idea on the trail, but now all I want to do is get back on the road."

"So you're leaving?"

"Yeah."

Daniel smiled and shook Jonathan's hand. "Good luck on your journey."

"It's just a vacation."

Daniel's smile widened. "Of course."

As Jonathan walked off toward his car, Daniel walked back to Carla's blanket. When he reached the blanket, he found Carla sitting upright with her arms posted at her sides and her legs stretches out in front of her.

"How'd it go?" Daniel asked.

"Smooth," Carla replied. "Paul's a cool guy."

"That he is," Daniel said. "Mind if I rest my head on your lap?"

"Go right ahead."

Daniel stretched out and laid his head on Carla's lap.

"Where's your friend?"

"He took off."

Twenty minutes later, as Carla was gently running her fingers through his hair, Daniel reached up and gripped her hand. He opened his eyes and took a deep breath. "I'm feeling something."

"How long has it been since you dropped?"

Daniel looked at his watch—it was 4:35 p.m. "Almost two hours."

Carla huffed. "I hope my high doesn't lag that much!"

"You can never tell with these things," Daniel said as he closed his eyes and took another deep breath. "Responses vary."

the caretaker

The Grateful Dead gave their first public performance of "Bird Song" on February 19, 1971, at the Capital Theater in Port Chester, New York. The song appeared in the second set, followed "Johnny B. Goode" and preceded "Easy Wind." Wallace Anzler knows this because he was there.

Ever since the first time he heard it live, "Bird Song" had struck a deep and pleasant chord in Wallace's heart. Its melodic tone and simple verses spoke to him, and, after hours of listening, it ultimately became his favorite Grateful Dead song. So, when he heard the song being sung by the naked young man wandering aimlessly through the woods of the resort he managed, his apprehensions were slightly eased.

"Hey there, good buddy," Wallace called out. "I'm the night manager here at the Eel River Resort. Are you one of our guests?"

The young man didn't respond to Wallace's question, just continued to wander about and sing. "If you hear that same sweet song again, will you know why? Anyone who sings a tune so sweet is passin' by."

Because Wallace wasn't quite sure if the young man was ignoring him or simply unaware of his presence, he cupped his hands around his mouth, walked a few steps closer, and repeated, "Are you one of our guests?"

Again, the man didn't respond. "Laugh in the sunshine, sing, cry in the dark, fly through the night…"

Throughout the four years Wallace worked as the night manger of the Eel River Resort, he'd encountered and dealt with many a drunk and disorderly guest. Having to do so was a part of his job, and he accepted the responsibility without complaint. But his encounter with this young man was different. His behavior wasn't that of someone who'd indulged in too much alcohol. It was the behavior of someone who'd indulged in something stronger and far more mentally invasive. Something that Wallace had once regularly indulged in himself but had since sworn to never touch again.

"Are you tripping?" Wallace asked in a steady voice.

Apparently the question awakened something in the young man, because he stopped singing and turned to face Wallace.

Encouraged by the sudden shift in behavior, Wallace waited patiently for a verbal response.

The man said nothing.

"I'll ask you one more time," Wallace said, "and if you don't answer me, I'm afraid I'm going to have to call the police. Are you tripping?"

The man shuffled closer to Wallace.

Startled, Wallace lifted his flashlight from the forest floor and shone it into the young man's eyes.

Both of his pupils remained dilated, allowing a painful amount of light to strike his retina. Still, he didn't flinch.

The illumination allowed Wallace to get his first good look at the man. He was pale and fright-stricken and his cheeks were stained with the streaks of dried tears.

"Tripping?" the young man questioned in a horse and barely audible voice.

"Yes," Wallace replied.

"I am...and I'm afraid I've lost my mind."

"I've been were you are," Wallace said calmly, "and I can tell you, a sure sign you haven't lost your mind is the fear that you have."

Tears began to slip from the young man's eyes. "Can you help me?"

"I not only can," Wallace replied, "I will."

By the time Wallace had gathered the man's clothes and guided him to his cabin, it was nearly nine o'clock. Initially, he'd planned to clothe him and then hand him off to whomever it was that he was with. But, after discovering the man's wallet and looking at the name on his driver's license, he learned that "Jonathan Normal" was not a guest, nor the companion of a guest, at the Eel River Resort.

Still, Wallace knew from experience that all Jonathan needed for a full recovery was time and kindness. So, for reasons only he completely understood, he decided to provide both.

"There you go," Wallace said to Jonathan as he tucked him into bed. "Are you comfortable now?"

"Comfortable?" Jonathan questioned.

"Yes," Wallace said as he stepped back from the bed, "You asked me to help make you comfortable. So I gave you a pair of pajamas to wear."

"Whose bed am I in?" Jonathan asked as he gripped the edge of the sheets and slid down slowly until only his eyes and the top of his head were exposed.

"Mine," Wallace said as he picked up a wooden chair, spun it around backward, and sat down. "You asked me if you could rest in it and I said yes."

Jonathan slid up to a seated position and smiled. "That's right, I did!" His face soured. "But, I also asked you for a bowl of Rice Crispies."

Wallace took a breath. "And I already told you. I didn't have any."

"You did?"

"Yes. I did... Do you remember when you dosed?"

"Dosed?" Jonathan questioned.

"When you took the drug you're on?" Wallace reiterated.

"Today!" Jonathan replied enthusiastically.

"'Today,'" Wallace repeated under his breath. "Thanks, that's helpful."

Jonathan's disposition confirmed that he was likely still hours away from a rational exchange of words. So Wallace braced himself for what he figured would be a long night.

"When I was a kid," Jonathan suddenly said, "I almost got the chance to drive a red Corvette."

"That's something," Wallace commented.

Jonathan smiled. "I was staying at my grandma's house in Everett."

"Everett, Washington?"

Jonathan shot Wallace a look. "I was talking."

"I'm sorry," Wallace said. "Please continue."

"My mom and dad were on vacation, so my grandma was looking after me. I liked my grandma's house but her dryer didn't work. So twice a week, I had to take our wet clothes down the street and dry 'em at the laundromat." He yawned. "One day, while I was drying our clothes, I heard a clanking sound in one of my dryers. At first I thought the clanking sound was money. So I pulled the clothes out of the dryer and looked inside. But money wasn't making the clanking sound." Jonathan stopped talking and stared off at a table near Wallace. "What's that?"

"This?" Wallace asked as he picked up a stuffed Jerry Garcia doll that was leaning up against a vase of dried flowers.

"Yeah," Jonathan replied.

"It's a doll."

"Could I hold it?"

"Sure," Wallace said as he tossed the doll onto Jonathan's lap. "It was a gift from my wife."

Jonathan looked around the cabin. "Where's you wife now?" he asked as he hugged the doll tightly.

"She's away."

"Far away?"

"Very far way..."

"Will she be back soon?"

"She won't," Wallace said as he reached over and thoughtfully rotated his wedding ring. "But, after a long life lived, I'll be with her again."

"Is she beautiful?"

Wallace took a deep breath, leaned forward, and rested his forearms on the back of his chair. "I don't feel up to talking about my wife right now. But I'd love to hear the rest of your story."

"What story?"

"You were telling me about a clanking sound in a dryer."

"I was?"

"You were."

"I'm sorry," Jonathan said in a soft voice, as he slid his body down and rested his head on the pillow beneath him. "I don't remember."

"That's okay," Wallace said. "Maybe you should try and get some sleep."

With eyes his open, Jonathan remained still and silent for the next fifteen minutes.

"How are things going for ya'?" Wallace asked.

"Fine," Jonathan replied. "Just thinking."

Wallace leaned up leaned up in his chair and stretched his back. "About what?"

"About the keys I found in the dryer."

"What about the keys?"

"They were the keys to a sports car."

"A red Corvette," Wallace said

Jonathan smiled at Wallace. "How did you know?"

Wallace winked. "I'm psychic."

"The Corvette was parked a few blocks from my grandma's house. It'd been there for two days and nobody knew whose it was, or why it never moved. But I did—"

"How did you know?" Wallace interjected.

"Because the owner couldn't drive it away."

"Because you had the keys."

"Right!"

Wallace smiled. "Please, go on."

"Later that night, I sneaked out of my grandma's house, walked over to the Corvette, and opened it."

"What happened then?"

"I sat inside."

"And?" Wallace prompted.

"It was a stick."

"So?"

"I don't know how to drive a stick."

"So, that's it?"

Jonathan huffed. "No… I remembered that Bryan, the kid who lived next door to my grandma, once bragged about having driven a stick. So I went to his house and tapped on his bedroom window. I told him about the car, about the keys I'd found, and how we'd both be able to say we drove a red Corvette if he'd come along with me."

"And this kid Bryan was up for that?"

"Bryan was totally up for it!" Jonathan replied enthusiastically. "So I told him to get dressed and meet me by the car. But while I was sitting on the street, waiting for Bryan, two men drove up in a truck. One of the men had a thin piece of metal that he used it to open the Corvette door. Then he fiddled around inside the car until it started. Then the other man got into the Corvette and drove away. Bryan came out a few minutes later."

"What did you tell him?"

"I told him what'd happened, but he didn't believe me. He called me a liar and punched me in the face."

Wallace winced.

"The next morning my grandma asked me why my cheek was bruised. I told her it'd happened while I was dreaming."

"Why didn't you show Bryan the keys you had?"

Jonathan didn't respond.

"Jonathan?" Wallace questioned as he sat up in his chair to get a closer look at his face. "Why didn't—" Wallace stopped talking.

Jonathan was sleeping.

Over the course of the next three hours, Jonathan bounced back and forth between bouts of undirected storytelling and brief episodes of silence. From there on out, he slept—awakening with a forceful stretch just before sunrise. "What time is it?"

"Five-forty-five," Wallace replied from across the room as he poured sugar into a cup of coffee. "Do you know where you are?"

Jonathan looked around the cabin. "Not really."

"You're at the Eel River Resort. The cabin you're in is mine."

"What city I'm I in?"

"Leggett."

"I'm sorry," Jonathan said, "but I don't remember your name."

"Wallace Anzler. I'm the night manager at the resort." Wallace picked up his coffee press and started to fill another cup. "Do you like cream or sugar in your coffee?"

"Both please," Jonathan replied as he sat up in bed. "My name's Jonathan Normal."

"Good to meet ya," Wallace replied as he prepared Jonathan's cup of coffee.

"How did I get here?"

Wallace walked over and handed Jonathan his cup. "You were spotted wandering naked in the woods nearby. I was sent to check on you. Once I realized you weren't in any condition to take care of yourself, I took you here."

Jonathan looked down into his cup of coffee. "I was naked?"

"As a bluebird," Wallace replied as he walked back to the other side of the room.

"Should I be apologizing?"

"Not at all," Wallace said with a smile. "Considering the state you were in, your behavior was appropriate. However, I'm curious."

"Yeah?"

"What exactly were you on?"

Jonathan let out a hard sigh. "Acid."

"I thought so," Wallace commented between sips of his coffee. "I swore it off years ago, myself."

"If I never do it again, it'll be too soon."

Wallace raised his cup of coffee into the air as if presenting a toast. "Good to hear."

"Say, Wallace."

"Yeah?"

"Why didn't you call the cops?"

"On you?"

"Yeah."

Wallace thought for a moment. "Karma."

"I don't understand."

"Back in '74, I found myself in a similar position to the one you were in last night."

"How old were you?"

"Twenty-four, twenty-five…"

"What happened?"

"I'd dropped acid during a Dead show in Oakland."

"What's a dead show."

"The Grateful Dead," Wallace clarified.

"Ah…" Jonathan replied knowingly. "The Grateful Dead. I've heard of them."

Wallace shrugged off Jonathan's inconsistent knowledge of the Dead and continued on. "So there I was, tripping my ass off, when I wandered out of the show and onto the streets outside. I'd gone to the show with friends, but they were tripping too, and had no idea I'd left their side, let alone the building. Alone, peaking on acid, scared shitless and on the verge of completely freaking out, Bill stepped up and helped me."

"Who's Bill?"

"Bill was a homeless guy who snatched me back from the curb just as I was about to walk into traffic. I was so out of my gourd I'd thought I was walking through a parking lot. Bill saw that I couldn't do much for myself, so he took me back to his shelter, covered me with blankets, and watched over me until my head cleared. The next morning, after my trip settled, he handed me a cup of coffee, wished me luck and sent me on my way."

Jonathan took a sip of his coffee. "Did you ever see Bill again?"

"I tried to thank him a few weeks later. But when I returned to the place his shelter had been, he and all his stuff were gone."

"So helping me was some kind of payback?"

"Something like that."

Jonathan took a breath. "I don't remember much about last night. Is that unusual?"

"To forget things you did while high?"

"Yeah."

"It's slightly usual, but it does happen."

"How was I?" Jonathan paused. "Last night that is?"

"You were fine," Wallace said. "Once I got you back here, you pretty much sat in that bed and told stories. Some I understood, some not. Then about twelve o'clock, you fell asleep. While you were sleeping, you mumbled things."

"What kind of things?"

"I couldn't understand most of the time. But at one point you talked about a guy named Bobby Ray."

Jonathan choked on his coffee.

"Are you okay?"

Jonathan cleared his throat and took a breath. "What exactly did I say?"

Wallace thought for moment. "You asked Bobby Ray to leave you alone."

"How-w-w did I ask that?" Jonathan stuttered. "What did I say?"

Wallace gulped nervously. "You said, 'Leave me alone, Bobby Ray.'"

Jonathan's face turned white. He looked uneasy and he started scratching his neck.

"Is something wrong?"

Jonathan pulled the sheets off his legs. "Do you have a bathroom?"

"Yes," Wallace said, pointing to the door beside him.

Jonathan got out of bed and set his coffee down on the floor. He walked over to the bathroom, went inside, and shut the door behind him.

"Is there anything I can get you?" Wallace asked.

"No, thanks," Jonathan called back. "I'll only be a minute!"

Wallace waited.

Five minutes later, Wallace heard his shower start.

Ten minutes after that, Jonathan called out. "Are these my clothes?"

"Everything I found in the area you were walking is stacked up on the hamper."

Jonathan emerged a short time later wearing his clothes and holding his keys. His hair was damp. "I used your towel," he said.

"That's all right," Wallace replied.

"I faintly remember parking my car near a large rock peppered with divots."

Jonathan's description sounded a lot like Indian Rock—a large granite bolder that the local Indians had once ground acorns upon. Wallace knew the place well. "I know where you're talking about," he said. "It's close to the freeway. I'll take you there."

Wallace walked alongside Jonathan down the redwood-lined trail that led to Indian Rock. The morning sun filtered through the dense canopy of branches and needles above them.

"How long have you lived in Leggett?" Jonathan asked, breaking a stretch of silence that had fallen between him and Wallace.

"Almost four years," Wallace replied.

"So you're relatively new to these parts?"

"I'm new to the area, but my great-great-grandfather, Peter Anzler, lived here back in the late 1800s. He's a bit of a legend in these parts."

Jonathan snapped a frond off a redwood tree and started plucking one leaf at a time. "Why's he a legend?"

Wallace thought for a moment. "Back in 1878, so one story goes, there was a fierce week-long storm that flushed so much water into the Eel River Valley that most of the countryside we're walking through now was flooded. Trees were ripped from the ground, bridges collapsed, and bank-side homes were torn from their foundations.

"My grandpa Peter was in one of those homes and was drifting down the Eel before he awoke and discovered his dilemma. But, on account of the speed he was moving, there wasn't anywhere safe he could get to without killing himself first. So he held on tight and prayed. After thirty minutes of house surfing, he started to hear the roar of the ocean. Shortly after that, his house came to a sudden stop on a sandbar at the base of the river.

"Smart enough to seize the moment, he picked himself up off the floor and jumped out a window. Moments later, the house dislodged from the sandbar and was crushed in the waves of the ocean."

Just as Wallace finished telling his story, he and Jonathan arrived at Indian Rock. Jonathan's car was parked nearby.

"Well," Jonathan said as he tossed the frond he was holding to the ground. "I suppose this is it."

"I suppose so," Wallace replied. "Take care of yourself and try to stay out of trouble."

"I'll try," Jonathan commented as he reached out and shook Wallace's hand.

"Where're you heading from here?" Wallace asked.

"Arcata, to visit a friend... After that I'm continuing on up the coast."

"What for?"

"I'm on a road trip."

"Planning to visit your grandma in Everett?"

"Everett?"

"Everett, Washington," Wallace clarified.

Jonathan paused. "My dad's mom died before I was born and my Grandma Nunez lives in San Diego."

"No relatives in Everett?"

Jonathan's face stiffened. "Why do you ask?"

Wallace smiled awkwardly. "You were spinning tales last night about a grandmother in Everett."

Jonathan took a deep breath and ran his fingers through his hair.

"People say odd things when they're high," Wallace said in a tender voice. "Try not to worry about it."

Jonathan looked at Wallace and sighed. "Thanks."

"You're welcome," Wallace said as he waved good-bye.

A few moments later, as Wallace was passing Indian Rock, he heard Jonathan start his engine and drive away.

the GOOD
CHRISTIAN

the good christian

Martin Dearborn was a consistent creature of habit. So long as he wasn't out of town, those who knew him best could find him within thirty minutes of an effort to do so. He woke up at the same time every day, ate the same breakfast every morning, and worked the same hours every week. In turn, nine o'clock Monday morning meant Martin was entering the third hour of his regular shift at the Arcata Co-op—the place he'd worked since moving to Arcata, California back in 1993.

"Jonathan!" Martin called out as he looked up from the pile of apples he was sorting. "What are you doing here?"

"Looking for you," Jonathan replied with a glowing smile. He reached out and hugged Martin. "I'd have called, but I lost your number."

Martin hugged Jonathan back. "What brings you to Arcata?"

"I needed a vacation, so I decided to take a road trip up the coast."

"Are you sticking around?" Martin asked as he stepped back.

"Just passing through…"

Martin shook his head and smiled. "Look at you."

Jonathan paused, still smiling. "What?"

"Are you in a band?"

Jonathan's smile flattened. "Why do you ask?"

"You're dressed head to toe in black!"

"So?"

Martin reached out and rested a hand on each of Jonathan's shoulders. "It's a good look. I like it."

Jonathan squinted and cocked his head to the side. "Are you serious, or are you just screwing with me?"

Martin dropped his hands back to his sides. "The last time I saw you, you were wearing a brown wool sweater and a pair of rip-kneed jeans."

Jonathan smiled. "I loved that sweater, but black suits me better these days."

"Hm," Martin said. "You'll have to tell me why that is over lunch."

Jonathan closed his eyes and placed an index finger on each of his temples. "Let me guess… Twelve o'clock, spinach salad at the Daybreak Café?"

"Am I that predictable?"

Jonathan opened his eyes and smiled. "You are, but it's comforting."

At twelve o'clock sharp, Martin walked up to the Daybreak Café. Once inside, he looked around for Jonathan but didn't see him. Pressed for time, he ordered his food and ate alone. As he was leaving the restaurant, on his way back to work, Jonathan walked up to him.

"Martin," Jonathan said as he raked his fingers through his hair. "I am so sorry."

"It's cool," Martin said as he shrugged his shoulders and continued walking on past Jonathan. "We'll catch up another time."

Jonathan stepped in front of Martin. His forehead was furrowed and his eyes looked sad. "Please, listen!"

Martin stopped walking and looked down at his wristwatch—it was 12:45 p.m. "My shift starts up again in fifteen minutes."

"I fell asleep in my car."

Martin smiled a soft, loving smile. "Jonathan."

"Yeah?"

"Really... It's okay."

Jonathan took a breath. "I just feel bad."

"It's not a problem." Martin paused. "Where are you staying?"

Jonathan paused. "The back seat of my car."

Martin pulled a pair of keys out of his front pocket and held them out toward Jonathan. "These are the keys to my house, the same one we lived at back in '93. Your room's a guestroom now. Use it."

"You live alone?" Jonathan said as he took hold of Martin's keys.

"I live with Osa."

"You two are still together?"

67

"We're married."

Jonathan smiled. "You married Osa!"

Martin nodded. "A year ago... Yes."

Jonathan reached out and tapped one of Martin's shoulders. "Congratulations!"

Martin glanced at his wristwatch. "Look, I gotta go," he said as he started walking away. "Let yourself into the house, settle into your room, and take a proper nap."

"Is Osa at the house?" Jonathan asked.

"No," Martin said as he spun around to face Jonathan, walking backward. "But our Bible study group's arriving at five o'clock."

"Bible study group?" Jonathan questioned disbelievingly.

"Help Osa set up when she gets in," Martin called out as he continued walking. "I'll call and let her know you're gonna be there!" He spun back around and ran off to work.

Martin's workday ended at three o'clock. On his way to the gym, he called Osa.

"How's your day going?" Martin asked Osa over the phone.

"Good. I'm on my way to the store to pick up food for tonight."

"Great," Martin said and then paused. "You remember Jonathan Normal?"

"The weird guy you lived with your freshman year in college?"

Martin paused. "Yeah..."

"What about him?"

"He's at the house sleeping in our guestroom."

"Why?"

"He's on a road trip up the coast. As he was passing through, he decided to pay me a visit. He looked tired, so I offered our guestroom as a place to nap."

"He just showed up out of the blue?"

"At the co-op this morning, yeah."

"When was the last time you two talked?"

Martin thought for a moment. "Five years ago."

Osa paused. "And you're comfortable with him being at our house alone?"

"Jonathan's a good guy, Osa."

"If you say so."

"What's that supposed to mean?"

"He gives me the creeps."

"Look, he's my friend. So rather than see him sleep in his car, I offered our guestroom. It was the right thing to do."

Osa sighed. "Are you on your way to the gym?"

"I'm out front now."

"Get on with your workout. I'll welcome Jonathan."

Martin pursed his lips. "Thanks, hon…I love you."

"I love you, too," Osa replied. "Just call before you do something like this again."

"I will… See you at four thirty."

As soon as Martin arrived home, he started helping Osa prepare food for the study group. "Is he still sleeping?" he asked, setting out a bowel of freshly made hummus.

"I suppose so," Osa replied. "The door's been shut since I got home."

"He looked pretty worn when I saw him this morning; I guess he needs the rest."

An hour and a half later, Martin was sitting in his living room. Circled around him were Osa and six other study group members. He opened his Bible, cleared his throat, and started to read John 3:16. "For God so loved the world that he gave—"

A loud moan emanated from behind the guestroom door.

Martin looked toward the guestroom and then looked back down at his Bible. He repeated, "For God so loved the world that he gave his one and only Son—"

"No!" Jonathan screamed, and then started weeping. "I'm gonna tell daddy and he's gonna make you stop. He's gonna make you stop!"

Martin calmly closed his Bible and stood up. "Excuse me for a moment. I'll be right back." He walked over to the guestroom door and knocked. "Jonathan," he called out as he looked back at the study group—smiling awkwardly at the stunned looks on their faces.

Jonathan moaned again.

"Check on him!" Osa whispered.

Martin took a breath and opened the door.

Inside, Jonathan was whimpering aloud, still apparently sleeping. "Please don't, please... Not again, please."

Martin reached out and shook Jonathan awake.

Jonathan's eyes slowly rolled open. He looked at Martin and smiled. "What time is it?"

Martin looked down at his wristwatch. "Six-twenty."

Jonathan stretched and yawned.

"Jonathan, you—" Martin stopped himself short and looked back toward the open guestroom door. He thought about telling Jonathan what it was he'd been saying in his sleep, but then considered the situation and the people waiting for him in the other room.

"What?" Jonathan questioned.

Martin took a breath. "Our study group is about to wrap up. Would you like to join us for the closing?"

Jonathan sat up in bed. He was in the same clothes Martin had seen him in earlier that day, minus his shoes. "My clothes are all wrinkled," he said as he picked at his shirt.

"We don't have a dress code." Martin reached out and took Jonathan's hand. "Come on… We're good people."

Jonathan shrugged his shoulders and smiled. "Okay."

Martin walked back into the living room, Jonathan shuffling in beside him.

Jonathan smiled and leaned in toward Martin's ear. "You're studying the Bible?"

"We are," Martin replied as he put a hand on one of Jonathan's shoulders. "Group, this is Jonathan. He'll be sitting with us for what remains of the meeting."

The group members greeted Jonathan with a disjointed, "Hi, Jonathan."

"Hi," Jonathan replied softly.

Osa smiled uncomfortably. "Hi, Jonathan."

Jonathan pointed at Osa and smiled. "Oh, hey, Osa!"

Osa adjusted her hair and looked away.

Martin pulled out a folding chair and added it to the circle of chairs in the living room. "Here you go, Jonathan."

"Thanks," Jonathan said as he sat down. His hair, which at its best was messy, reached up as if it was about to high-five the person next to him.

Martin sat down back down in his seat, placing a hand on each of his knees. "Given the time, let's move on to final statements." He looked across the circle at a short, thin man wearing a white t-shirt and a jean jacket. "Russell, you had something you wanted to share."

Russell pinched his lips tightly and nodded. "My father was born and raised in a town called Hope. It's about 100 miles east of Vancouver, British Columbia." Russell paused. "Just outside Hope is Harrison Lake. It was there my father camped, learned to swim, and ice fished during the winter. It was also where he met my mother, and where her ashes were scattered after she died." Russell stopped talking, tears making his eyes glisten.

The study group members sitting to Russell's left and right each placed a hand on one of his shoulders.

Russell wiped the tears from his eyes. "Thank you, I'm fine."

As the hands left Russell's shoulders, he took a breath. "While I stood beside my father as he spread my mother's ashes, he looked at me and said, 'One day, you'll do this for me.'" He took another breath. "A week ago, my father passed away in his sleep. He was sixty-four." Russell sniffled. "So, tomorrow I'm flying out to Vancouver with his ashes. Then, I'm renting a car and driving out to Harrison Lake to scatter my farther along the banks of the place he loved most. The place he said 'all things worth remembering' occurred."

"Blessed be your trip," one of the group members said.

"May the hand of our Lord be pressed upon your shoulder," another group member said.

"Yes," Martin followed. "Our hearts and prayers will be with you." Martin paused. "Please everyone, join hands."

Everyone in the circle reached out for the hand next to theirs, except for Jonathan.

"We're about to say our closing prayer, Jonathan. You're welcome to join us."

Jonathan stood up and sat down on a couch outside the circle. "Sorry."

"Don't be," Martin said. "It's fine."

The group members joined hands, closing the circle.

Jonathan sat quietly as Martin lead the group in the Lord's Prayer.

"Remember," Martin said as he let go of the hands of the person next to him and raised his head, "next week we'll be discussing Christ's humiliation and exaltation. So be sure to read Philippians, paying special attention to chapter two, lines five through eleven."

The tone of the group abruptly shifted from one of formality to one of relative ease. All stood up and began to mingle freely.

"I was touched by what you said earlier," Jonathan said to Russell a few minutes later.

"Thanks," Russell replied. "My father and I were pretty close."

"If you don't mind me asking, how—"

"Heart attack," Russell interjected.

"I'm so sorry… But, that's not what I was about to ask."

"Oh?"

"I was just curious, how old are you?"

"Twenty-one… I'll be twenty-two in three months."

"I don't think I could handle what you must be going through."

"You'd handle it just like you're handling life right now— moment to moment, day by day."

Jonathan paused. "You think that's how I'm handling life?"

Russell smiled. "Such is the way people live when they're searching."

Jonathan smiled uncomfortably. "What are you talking about?"

"Your journey."

Jonathan's smile flattened. "You're the second person to tell me I'm on a 'journey.' What's that about?"

"Truth," Russell replied cheekily and then walked off.

"I'm on vacation!" Jonathan said sternly to Russell's back.

Russell didn't respond. He continued walking away from Jonathan and toward a cluster of study group members. After receiving a barrage of hugs and well wishes, he headed toward the front door. On his way past Jonathan, he said, "Good luck."

"I'm not searching for anything!" Jonathan snapped back.

As Russell held open the front door, he looked back at Jonathan one last time. "Sure," he said, and then walked outside and shut the door behind him.

Jonathan looked dazed.

"Try not to be put off by Russell," Martin said as he stepped up to Jonathan. "He means well."

Jonathan huffed. "He comes off as obnoxious!"

Martin waved goodbye to the last study group member to leave, and then looked back at Jonathan. "How does dinner and beers at the Humboldt Brewery sound to you?"

Jonathan's face lit up slightly. "I'm game for that. Just let me straighten up a bit before we head out."

"No problem. You know were the bathroom is."

Jonathan smiled.

While Jonathan was in the bathroom, Osa approached Martin in the kitchen. He was washing dishes. "Did you talk to Jonathan about his outburst?" she asked.

"No," Martin replied. "I get the feeling he doesn't have the faintest idea he was talking in his sleep."

"Was he awake when you walked in?"

"No."

Osa looked away from Martin and sighed. "He makes me nervous."

Martin set down the dish he was holding and turned off the sink water. "Osa, he's my friend."

"You only knew him a year," Osa said under her breath.

"'Your friends will know you better in the first minute you meet than your acquaintances will know you in a thousand years.'"

Osa rolled her eyes. "Don't quote Richard Bach at me," she said as she started walking out of the kitchen.

"We're walking to the brewery for dinner and beers," Martin called out.

"Have a hoot!" Osa called back.

"So how long has it been?" Martin asked Jonathan on their way to the brewery.

"Since I was last in Arcata?" Jonathan asked.

"Yeah."

"I haven't set foot in this town since I dropped out of Humboldt State back in…1994. So it's been…what, five years?"

"Five years," Martin replied in confirmation. "Speaking of school, why did you drop out? I never understood that. Your grades were strong."

"My head just wasn't into it, so I figured I'd take a year off and work for a while. But one thing led to another, and I started making money. Money led to bills, bills led to debt, and before I knew it, college just wasn't an option anymore." Jonathan paused. "When did you graduate?"

"'97."

"Psychology, right?"

"Yeah."

"Are you planning to use your degree?"

Martin smiled. "I use it every day."

"Are you planning to make a living at it?" Jonathan clarified.

"Eventually… But for now, working at the co-op suits me fine."

Jonathan nodded knowingly. "I get that." He walked in silence for a moment. "What's up with the Bible studies?"

"What do you mean?"

"You never struck me as a religious guy."

"Osa and I broke up our senior year in college. At the time, we'd been growing apart for months and the end was understandable. Still, the separation was tough on us both. To ease the transition, I sought solace in the Bible, eventually joining a Christian fellowship on campus. To my surprise, Osa was a member, having sought comfort in the Bible herself. From that point on, we devoted our lives to Christ. We married a year after that."

"You and Osa are born-again Christians?"

Martin smiled. "Yes."

Jonathan smiled and shook his head. "Things change."

Once inside Humboldt Brewery, Jonathan and Martin settled into a wooden booth near the bar.

As Martin picked up his menu, Jonathan leaned forward and asked, "What happened to Martin the rebel? The pirate radio DJ?"

"He's still in me," Martin said as he looked over his menu. "I'm just not angry anymore."

A few moments later, a waitress visited Martin and Jonathan's table, took their orders for beer and food, and walked away.

"When was the last time you did radio?" Jonathan asked.

"My sophomore year."

"Why'd you stop?"

"F.A.R. closed."

"F.A.R.?"

"Free Arcata Radio."

"Ah… Never heard it called F.A.R."

"Hrm," Martin grunted.

"Ever think of grabbing a slot on 94.9 or KHUM?"

"Once it looked like 94.9 was gonna stick around for a while, I thought about it, but never pushed on the idea."

"What about KHUM?"

"What about it?"

"Did you ever think of working there?"

"You've got to be kidding!" Martin sat back in his seat. "KHUM may claim they're 'radio without the rules,' but don't believe it. It's college radio, which means it's primarily government funded. They may not want to admit it, but they have rules."

"I suppose," Jonathan commented.

"Besides," Martin continued, "after experiencing the kind of freedom pirate radio afforded me, I couldn't imagine working at a licensed station."

Jonathan smiled. "Do you remember the time you said you were going to bring a cow to the plaza, encircle it in a Plexiglas barrier, slaughter it, grill it, and then feed it to whoever wanted a burger?"

Martin laughed. "My hidden-truths-behind-processed-foods rant."

"That was classic!"

"Eighty-two people showed up!"

Jonathan's smile grew. "I remember!"

Martin smiled. "People stood around for hours waiting for the cow to show."

"Laying out a tarp and setting up that Plexiglas wall the night before was a nice touch!"

"Thanks, I was especially proud of that." Martin paused. "You wouldn't believe the amount of mail I received from angry listeners."

"Oh, I remember... But were they angry because you goofed 'em or because you didn't slaughter the cow?"

"Both!"

The waitress returned. "Two pale ales."

"Awesome!" Martin exclaimed as he sat up in his seat.

Jonathan raised his glass. "To better days."

Martin lifted his beer and tapped Jonathan's glass. "Better days." He took a sip of his beer. "How is it?"

Jonathan finished his sip and set his drink down. "Just like I remember it."

Martin took a deep breath. "Say, Jonathan…"

"Yeah?"

"Earlier tonight—" Martin paused.

"Uh-huh?"

"When I woke you up," Martin continued trepidatiously.

Jonathan took another sip of his beer. "Right?"

"You were talking in your sleep."

Jonathan set his drink down, looking uncomfortable. "What did I say this time?"

"So you're aware you do this?"

"I'm aware I've been doing it lately, yeah."

"You sounded pretty upset."

"What did I say?" Jonathan repeated.

"You were pleading with someone. Telling them 'no' and 'I'm gonna tell daddy and he's gonna make you stop.'" Martin paused. "When I went in to check on you, you were crying, 'Please don't, please… Not again, please.'"

Jonathan stared off at his beer. "Did the people in your study group hear me?"

"They did."

"Great," Jonathan said in a flat voice.

"Do you have any idea what might be bringing this on?"

Jonathan reached out and took a sip of his beer. "I do."

"What?"

"I'm a mortuary driver," Jonathan said, and then paused.

"Go on?"

"Do you know what a mortuary driver does?"

"Picks up remains for a mortuary," Martin replied nonchalantly.

"Right."

"So?"

"So most people aren't okay with my job."

"Someone needs to pick 'em up," Martin commented in a vaguely indignant tone. "What does your work have to do with talking in your sleep?"

Jonathan cleared his throat. "Last Friday, I picked up a man named Robert Ray Lewis, and ever since, I've had recurring nightmares and I'm talking in my sleep."

"And you think this pickup has something to do with it?"

Jonathan finished off what was left of his beer. "I'm pretty positive it does, yeah."

"Why?"

"It's hard to explain… I just know."

Martin paused. "Did you know this person when he was alive?"

"Not that I can remember."

"And you're dreaming about him?"

"Not directly, but I feel his presence."

"What does his presence feel like?"

Jonathan reached up and absently scratched his neck. "Heavy… Suffocating."

Martin paused. "I hate to bring this up. Because on critical examination, the scientific evidence for it crumbles. But, have you ever heard Freud's theory of repression?"

"You mean repressed memories?"

"Yeah… How well do you understand them?"

"I saw an episode about 'em on Oprah."

Martin smiled. "Just in case Oprah was loose on her facts, the theory suggests that the mind automatically banishes traumatic events from memory to prevent overwhelming anxiety."

Jonathan picked up his empty glass as if to drink from it and then set it back down.

Martin continued. "Maybe you're repressing a traumatic childhood memory involving the man you picked up."

"I seriously don't remember meeting this guy before Friday."

"That's consistent with repression," Martin commented. "On the other hand, it's also consistent with never having met him before."

Jonathan paused. "Then what's your point?"

Martin shrugged his shoulders. "I don't know."

The waitress returned. "Two veggie burgers with fries!"

Martin and Jonathan thanked her, shifted their attention toward their food, and didn't say much to one another for the next twenty minutes that followed. After splitting the bill, they started walking back toward the house.

"Theoretically speaking," Jonathan said as he walked beside Martin, "if I did repress the memory of a childhood trauma, what could I do to help myself?"

"Theoretically speaking, repressed memories are stored in the unconscious mind, outside the awareness of the conscious mind. But time, therapy, and support can change that. Once you return awareness of the trauma, you can deal with the feelings involved."

"So I need therapy?"

"It couldn't hurt."

Jonathan wiped his hands over his face, looked up, and took a breath.

A few minutes later, Martin and Jonathan arrived back at the house. Martin walked in, but Jonathan paused outside the front door. "Thanks for the hospitality. I'm heading out from here."

Martin looked down at his wristwatch—it was 8:45 p.m. "Where are you going?"

"Up the coast... I have an old friend in Ashland I want to visit."

"Does he know you're coming?"

Jonathan rubbed the back of his neck. "No."

Martin shook his head. "You're something else... Do you have an overnight bag?"

"Why?"

"Because it's almost nine o'clock and there's no sense in heading out tonight. Call your friend, stay the night, and leave in the morning."

Jonathan paused.

"You're staying the night, Jonathan!"

Jonathan took a breath. "Okay, all right. I'll be back in a minute."

Ten minutes later, Jonathan returned to the house with a large black gym bag. "Can I use your phone?" he asked Martin as he walked in.

"There's one in the guestroom."

"Thanks," Jonathan said as he started walking toward the guestroom.

Martin cleared his throat loudly.

Jonathan paused. "What?"

"Are you planning to get up at five a.m.?"

"Not particularly."

"Then this is goodbye."

Jonathan nodded. "That's right... Your shift starts at six."

"Five days a week," Martin said as reached out and hugged Jonathan. "It was good to see you again."

"It was good seeing you too," Jonathan said as he stepped back. "Thanks for the hospitality."

Martin smiled. "You're welcome."

When Martin walked into his bedroom, he found Osa readied for sleep, sitting up in bed, reading. "Hi, hon," he said as he sat down beside her.

"Jonathan's spending the night," Osa said without looking away from her book.

"Are you mad?"

Osa put her book down. "Mostly at myself."

Martin's face softened. "Why?"

"Because you're a good Christian and I make you feel guilty about it."

"You don't make me feel guilty, hon."

Osa pursed her lips. "How was your dinner?"

"Good," Martin said as he started pulling his off his shoes. "But one thing's for sure."

"What's that?"

"Jonathan's troubled."

"Hasn't he always been?"

"Not like this," Martin commented as he gazed off toward the floor. "He's different now, darker."

Osa reached out and gripped one of Martin's hands.

Martin gently squeezed Osa's hand and then let go. "I'm okay." He stood up and walked toward the bathroom. "I'm gonna take a shower and get ready for bed. I'll see you in a bit."

Ten minutes later, Martin slid open the door to the bathroom. He smiled at Osa as he brushed his teeth.

Osa shook her head and smiled back at him. Her smile suddenly faded. "Martin."

"Mrph-huh?" Martin replied, still brushing his teeth.

"Listen!"

Martin spat out the toothpaste in his mouth, wiped his lips and paused. He could hear Jonathan crying.

Osa took a breath. "Do you think you should check on him?"

Martin started toward the guestroom. "I'll be right back."

From outside the closed guestroom door, Martin could hear Jonathan talking on the phone. Not wanting to intrude, he turned around and headed back to his bedroom.

"Is he okay?" Osa asked Martin as he walked in.

"He's talking on the phone."

"With who?"

Martin shrugged his shoulders. "I don't know."

Osa paused. "What time is he leaving tomorrow?"

"I'm not sure, after me sometime."

"So he and I'll be here alone together?"

"I suppose so, yeah."

Osa grimaced. "Would you mind if I left the house with you tomorrow morning?"

"Not at all."

"Thanks."

the parents

Doug and Brenda Normal felt like they had two sons in Jonathan. From birth to his eighth year of life he adored their company and showered them with admiration and love. But from his ninth birthday forward, he would have nothing to do with them. This shift in Jonathan's attitude toward them was sudden and emotionally devastating, increasing the rift that was already forming in Doug and Brenda's marriage. Still, out of habit, they stayed together, or at least that's what they told themselves. More truthfully, they stayed together for the hope that they shared. A hope that one day their son of old would return.

"Would you pick up the phone?" Brenda called out from inside the bathroom, as she vigorously scrubbed the sink.

Doug was reclined on a Barcalounger in the living room. He was holding a beer can in one hand and a remote control in the other. "Could you get it? I'm watching TV!"

"I can't!"

"Why not?"

"I'm cleaning!"

Doug sighed, dropped the remote, unreclined the chair, and set his beer can on the floor. As he started toward the kitchen phone, he grumbled under his breath. When he reached the phone, he snatched it up and pressed Talk. "Hello?"

There was silence on the line.

"Hello?" Doug repeated.

"Hi, Dad."

Doug's shoulders sank. "Jonathan?"

"Yeah, it's me."

"How've you been?"

There was a moment of silence on the line. "I've been better."

"You in trouble?"

"Now, why would you ask that?"

"We haven't heard from you in two years, Jonathan. What else am I supposed to think?"

"Well, I'm not in trouble," Jonathan replied in a noticeably irritated tone.

Doug took a breath. "Are you still working at the mortuary?"

"No."

"Why not?"

"I was fired."

"Why?"

Jonathan sighed. "I damaged some property. Look, I'm not calling to catch up."

Doug huffed. "Is that right?"

"Yeah," Jonathan snapped back, and then took a breath. "I have a question."

Doug shook his head. "Ask away."

"When I was a kid—" Jonathan paused.

"Yeah?"

"Did we know a man named Robert Ray Lewis?"

"A man named who?"

"Robert Ray Lewis. He was a black man. He might have been a friend of the family or an acquaintance? I'm not sure."

Doug thought for a moment. "Never heard of the guy."

"Are you sure?"

"Yes, I'm sure."

"How about Mom?"

"Jonathan, what's all this about?"

Brenda walked up to Doug. She was wearing blue rubber dish gloves and holding a damp sponge. "Is that Jonathan?" she asked. "I want to talk to him!"

Doug shot Brenda a look of irritation.

Brenda walked over to the kitchen sink, stripped off her gloves and dropped them, and the sponge she was holding, inside. Then she gestured for Doug to give her the phone. "Now, Doug!"

Doug lowered the phone to his chest and cupped a hand over the mouthpiece. "Hold on!" he whispered tersely. He brought the phone back up to his ear.

"What's going on?" Jonathan questioned.

"Nothing," Doug replied. "What's all this about, again?"

Jonathan paused. "I think I might have been molested by a man named Robert Ray Lewis."

Doug's chin dropped and his mouth gaped open.

"What is it?" Brenda asked. "What did he say?"

Doug handed Brenda the phone. "He thinks he was molested."

"When?" Brenda asked as she took hold of the phone.

"I don't know," Doug replied as he shook his head. "Ask him."

"Jonathan?" Brenda questioned into the phone.

"Hey, Mom," Jonathan replied.

"What is this about a molestation?"

Jonathan took a breath. "I think I was molested."

"When?"

"When I was kid."

Brenda paused. "Is this some kind of joke, Jonathan? Huh? Are you joking with us?"

"No..."

Brenda started to cry. "You used to be such a good kid, Jonathan. Now we don't hear from you for two years, and when you finally call, you call us with this! How could you? How could you say such a horrible thing?" She handed the phone back to Doug, stepped aside, and sobbed.

"Are you happy now?" Doug questioned sternly into the phone. "Your mother's crying."

"I'm not trying to make Mom cry, Dad."

"Well, you did!" Doug heard Jonathan explode into tears.

"I'm sorry," Jonathan blubbered, "I am. But I'm trying to make sense of a lot of things that aren't making sense right now. And things—"

"Jonathan," Doug interjected.

Jonathan didn't respond.

"Jonathan!"

Jonathan sniffled. "Yeah?"

"Get a grip. You know I can't stand it when both you and your mother are crying at the same time. I start to feel like an angry red tomato in a—"

"A tear sandwich," Jonathan interjected.

Doug's face softened. "Exactly."

Jonathan took a shuttering breath. "I'm sorry…"

"It's okay."

Jonathan paused. "So you never knew a man named Robert Ray Lewis?"

"I would tell you if we did," Doug replied calmly.

"He might have also gone by the name Bobby Ray."

"Jonathan," Doug warned.

"Yeah?"

"No."

Jonathan sniffled.

"You got that?"

"Yes," Jonathan replied timidly.

Doug took a breath. "Do you remember the time you got stuck in the storm channel?"

"Yeah."

"Did you know how worried I was that I was gonna loose you that day?"

"Come on, Dad. You were cool as a cucumber. I remember your eyes. They were steady and focused the whole time."

"They were steady and focused for you," Doug commented. "You're my son, Jonathan, your mother's and my only child. You're an adult now and can live your life as you see fit. But when you were young, your mother and I were your protectors. We hawked over everything you did. We gave you space to explore but stayed close enough to step in, pick you up, and dust you off, always."

"I know, Dad, and I appreciate that, really I do."

Doug paused. "Regardless of what's gotten into your head, you weren't molested as a child. Not on our watch. You understand?"

Jonathan sniffled. "I do."

"Let me talk to him," Brenda whispered as she reached out for the phone.

Doug handed Brenda the phone.

"Jonathan?"

"Yeah, Mom."

"Did you hear what your father said?"

Jonathan sighed. "Yes, Mom."

"It true... We'd never let anything like that happen to you."

"I get that, Mom."

Brenda took a breath. "Are you still living in the city?"

"Yeah. But I'm not there now."

"Where are you?"

"Arcata."

"What are you doing there?"

"Visiting Martin."

"Your roommate from college?"

"Yeah. I'm on a road trip up the coast. I was passing through, so I stopped by."

"How long are you staying in Arcata?"

"Just today… I'm heading out tomorrow morning."

"To where?"

"Ashland, to visit Joe."

"Do I know Joe?"

"Joe Rosenberg, Mom."

"Your friend from grade school?"

"Yeah."

"How is he?"

"I don't know, Mom, that's why I'm visiting him—to find out."

Brenda smiled. "When you two were kids, you were inseparable. When's he expecting you?"

Jonathan took a breath. "He isn't."

"What do you mean, 'He isn't'?"

"His sister gave me his address and phone number a few months back. She said he worked from home."

"So?"

"So, he'll be home."

Brenda sighed. "That's hardly the issue, Jonathan. Show some courtesy and call the man before you show up on his doorstep!"

"I'll call."

"When?"

"I don't know… Tonight."

Brenda huffed. "It's after nine o'clock!"

"So?"

"Don't you think it's a little a late to be calling people?"

"For you and Dad, maybe, but not for everybody."

"If you say so," Brenda commented dismissively. "Here's your father."

Doug took hold of the phone. "Jonathan."

"Yeah, Dad?"

"We want to turn your bedroom into an exercise space."

Jonathan paused. "Go for it."

Doug rolled his eyes. "I wasn't asking for your blessing Jonathan. I need you to come by and pick up your stuff."

"What stuff?"

"Your clothes, comics, pictures, yearbooks… That kind of stuff."

Jonathan paused. "I'll swing by the house when I'm back in the Bay Area."

"You're not in San Francisco?"

"He's in Arcata," Brenda called out from the bathroom. "Says he's on a road trip."

Jonathan sighed. "Look Dad, it's getting late. I've gotta get going."

Doug sighed. "Sure, sure…"

"Say goodbye to Mom for me."

"I will. But, one more thing."

"What's that?"

"When you swing by to pick up your stuff, could we all grab a bite to eat together—you, your mother, and me? If you're pressed for time, we could grab a cup of coffee."

"I could do dinner."

"Really?"

"Yeah."

"Great." Doug took a breath. "And—"

"Dad," Jonathan interjected. "I really gotta go."

"Okay… Take care of yourself."

"I will, Dad."

Doug hung up the phone.

"Are you done watching TV?" Brenda asked Doug as she whizzed by on her way toward the living room.

"Jonathan had to go," Doug called out. "But he wanted me to tell you good-bye." He heard the sound of a beer can striking the wall. "Everything okay?" he asked as he grimaced, pretty much knowing what had happened.

"I kicked your beer. How many times have I told you not to leave your cans on the floor!"

"Do you want me to clean it up?"

"No," Brenda replied. "I will!"

Doug sighed. "Of course."

the childhood friend

the childhood friend

Shortly after Joe Rosenberg's eighth birthday, his parents, Marshall and Julia, filed for divorce. Once the divorce was settled, Marshall moved back east to live with his brother, severing all contact with his former wife and kids. Julia continued living in Niles, California, supporting Joe and his older sister, Stephanie, on her own.

Following Joe's ninth birthday, his mother married a wastewater treatment technician named Ed Cook. Ed was a good man but focused singularly on Julia, never completely comfortable with Joe or Stephanie. That was the primary reason Stephanie opted to spend her senior year of high school living with a friend rather than move to Ashland, Oregon—the city where Ed had picked up a supervisory position. At the time of the move, Joe was ten and didn't have the option of staying with his sister. He was going to Ashland with Ed and his mother whether he liked it or not.

Joe attended college at the University of Oregon, in Eugene. His junior year in college, he married his then girlfriend, Valerie Luddon. Two years after graduating, he and Valerie divorced.

Heartbroken, Joe moved back to Ashland, where he'd been living off savings and unemployment checks ever since. He told his mother and his sister that he worked from home so they wouldn't hassle him about getting a job. For now at least, he didn't want one.

Joe was content with the consistency that his life afforded him, spending his days dressing up, listening to Cocteau Twins records, and feeding raisins to his companion and best friend, a pet chinchilla named Björk.

"Who wants a raisin?" Joe questioned in a childish voice as he bent over at the waist, a small box of raisins in one hand. "Huh?"

Björk rose up from her bed of cedar chips and scurried over to the front of the cage.

Joe pulled a raisin out of the box. "Does Björk want a raisin?"

Björk started to make a high-pitched squeaking sound akin to the one an inflated balloon makes when someone pinches its opening and lets the air out in short, consecutive bursts.

"What's that?" Joe questioned as he pushed a raisin through a small gap in Björk's cage.

The chinchilla took hold of the raisin, clutched it in her paws, and started eating.

"Björk wants a raisin," Joe said as he stood up straight and smiled. "Björk does."

The phone rang.

Joe looked across the living room and into the attached kitchen where the phone hung on a wall. He rested his hands on his hips and looked to Björk. "Are we home?"

Björk was singularly focused on eating her raisin.

The phone continued to ring.

Joe dropped his arms and sighed. "All right, all right," he said on his way to the phone. "I'm coming!" He picked the handset off the wall. "Hell-low?"

"Joe?"

Joe paused. "Who's this?"

"Jonathan Normal."

"Jonathan who?"

"Normal. It's been a while, but you and I were friends back in the day."

Joe's eyes lit up. "Oh my god!" he exclaimed. "Jonathan Normal! What's up?"

Jonathan cleared his throat. "I'm on a road trip and thought it'd be cool to swing by your apartment for a visit."

"You know where I live?"

"I bumped into your sister at a grocery store in San Francisco."

"She lives there," Joe commented.

"Yeah... She gave me your address and phone number."

"My address here in Ashland?"

"Yeah..." Jonathan paused. "Are you up for a visit?"

"Sure," Joe said. "When?"

"Tomorrow morning, around ten. Does that work for you?"

"I'll be home," Joe commented before thinking his words through. He paused and then stammered, "but, ah... I'm not..."

"Great, then," Jonathan cut in, "I'll see you tomorrow at ten. We'll grab brunch!"

"But I'm not—" Joe heard a dial tone on the line. He dropped his chin to his chest. A few seconds later, he hung up the phone, walked over to his living room couch, and sat down. He looked at Björk.

Björk looked back at him.

"Looks like we're gonna have a visitor," Joe said, and then sighed dramatically.

Björk sighed back.

At 10:15 a.m. the next day, Joe's doorbell chimed. After taking a deep breath, he walked up to the front door and looked through the peephole. He saw a man in an untucked black dress shirt adjusting his hair. Joe unlocked and opened the door. "Jonathan?" he questioned tentatively.

Jonathan dropped his hands to his sides and smiled. "Hey, Joe!"

Joe stepped back, smiled a subtle but noticeable smile, then opened the door wide. "Welcome."

Jonathan stepped into Joe's apartment and immediately started scanning around. A few moments later he commented, "Like the Cocteau Twins much?"

Joe's front door opened into a spacious rectangular living room covered floor to ceiling in framed Cocteau Twins flyers, tickets, album covers, photos, and posters. In the center of the room was a long coffee table covered with British music magazines and takeout menus. Beyond the coffee table was a TV in front of a narrow wall wedged between two doors. One door led to Joe's bedroom and the other to a bathroom. In front of the coffee table was a massive brown leather couch. At the end of the couch, nearest to the front door, was the cage inside which Björk lived. Behind the couch and Björk's cage was a half wall that separated the living room from the kitchen.

Joe shut the front door and sighed dramatically. "The Cocteau Twins feed me."

"Feed you?" Jonathan questioned.

"I like them a lot," Joe clarified as he gestured toward the couch. "Have a seat."

Jonathan sat down at the end of the couch closest to Björk's cage and continued looking around. "It looks like a shrine in here."

Joe sat down at the other end of the couch. He rested the palms of his hands on his lap and held his knees together, leaving a large gap between himself and Jonathan. "I like it."

Jonathan turned toward Joe and rested an arm atop the couch. "Don't get me wrong. I like it too. I just haven't seen this many photos of a single band in one place."

"One hundred and fifty-four," Joe said, "minus one."

Jonathan smiled awkwardly. "I'm sorry?"

Joe sighed again. "I have one hundred and fifty-four framed pieces in my living room. All of them have to do with the Cocteau Twins except that one." Joe pointed toward a framed photo above the TV. It was a candid shot of a woman in a gray business suit leaning back and laughing. She was an attractive woman with porcelain white skin, a small round face, short brown hair, and smoky eyes.

"I'm a fan," Jonathan commented dismissively. "I know who she is."

Joe locked eyes with Jonathan. "You know my ex-wife?"

Jonathan's brow raised in a look of astonishment. "You were married to the lead singer of the Cocteau Twins?"

Joe rolled his eyes. "That's not Elizabeth Fraser. That's my ex-wife, Valerie."

"Ah," Jonathan replied and then paused. "Why is there a photo of your ex-wife on the wall?"

Joe took a breath. "Let's just say things ended on her terms, not mine."

Jonathan grimaced. "Sorry."

"It's not a problem," Joe said flatly.

Jonathan leaned forward and fiddled with the magazines on the coffee table. "So, how you been?"

Joe looked up and squinted. "How have I been?" he said, thinking for a moment. "Better." He looked at Jonathan and flashed a weak smile. "I've been better."

Jonathan pursed his lips. "So, things aren't good?"

"Not really."

Jonathan rubbed the back of his neck and glanced toward the front door. "Look, if this is a bad time—"

"It's nothing like that," Joe interjected quickly. "You don't have to leave. It's just—" He stopped talking.

"Yeah?"

Joe's shoulders dropped. He leaned forward, rested his elbow on his thighs, turned, and looked at Jonathan. "Would you mind if I smoked some pot?"

"Not at all," Jonathan quickly replied. "Would you mind if I joined you?"

Joe smiled. "Not at all."

Twenty minutes later, Joe was standing in the kitchen, pulling milk and eggs out of the refrigerator. The Cocteau

Twins "Sugar Hiccup" filled the air, and he rolled his head from side to side to its waltz-like, ethereal melody.

Jonathan was sitting on the living room couch, holding a raisin out toward, but not into, Björk's cage. "Like this?" he questioned as he gestured with the raisin pinched between his forefinger and thumb.

Joe looked over at Jonathan and laughed.

Jonathan smiled. "What?"

"Poke it into the cage!"

Jonathan started giggling. "Oh, yeah, right." He poked the raisin into the cage.

Björk scurried over, grabbed the raisin between her paws, and started eating it.

"Look at her go!" Jonathan exclaimed.

"When it comes to raisins, Björk doesn't fuck around," Joe commented. He looked confused for a moment and scratched his head. "What was I was making again?"

"Scrambled eggs and bacon!" Jonathan exclaimed.

"Sor-ry!" Joe replied. "I forgot."

Jonathan smiled. "For the third time!"

Joe giggled.

Jonathan leaned forward and picked a pipe off the coffee table. "Can I take another hit?"

"Totally!" Joe said. "I've got lots."

"Awesome." Jonathan held the pipe up to his mouth and lit the bowl.

As Jonathan inhaled, Joe set the milk and eggs back into the refrigerator and closed the door. He took a breath, left the kitchen, crossed the living room and paused in front of his bedroom door. "Jonathan," he said.

"Yeah?" Jonathan questioned, exhaling a puff of smoke and coughing.

"I'm gonna change. Is that okay?"

Jonathan took a moment to catch his breath. "Change what?"

"My clothes."

Jonathan set the pipe back onto the coffee table. "Whatever."

Joe gripped the doorknob to his bedroom and looked back at Jonathan. "Are you sure?"

Jonathan pressed his fingertips against his temples and closed his eyes. "Let me think about it..." He popped his eyes open and smiled. "Yes!"

Joe smiled. "Then I'll be right back!" He opened the door to the bedroom and disappeared behind the other side.

Joe's bedroom looked as if a theater arts makeup studio and the bedroom of a teen princess had collided with one another. To the left of the door, an unmade queen-sized bed with deep red sheets sat between two massive wardrobes. Both wardrobes were stuffed to the brim with a colorful array of stylish gowns, skirts, and blouses. And, although Joe would insist that he needed every one of them, the floors of the wardrobes were cluttered with an absurd number of women's shoes. To the right of the door, opposite the wardrobes and the bed, was a white art deco vanity. The vanity boasted a circular mirror framed between two rounded posts—a wig atop each—and a countertop covered in makeup containers.

As soon as Joe entered the bedroom, he immediately started pulling off his clothes.

Once naked, he dug through a wardrobe, pulled out a white silk blouse and a pair of silk panties and slid them both on. Then he pulled out a conservative women's suit and a pair of shoes. The suit was light gray, with a three-button, mid-hip length jacket and matching gray skirt. The shoes were black, two-inch heels.

After putting on and adjusting the suit, Joe stood in front of his vanity mirror and admired how proper he looked—like a good English woman should, he thought to himself.

"Do you mind if I take *another* hit off your weed?" Jonathan called out from the living room.

"Smoke as much as you want," Joe replied as he sat down on his vanity chair.

"Thanks!"

Joe powdered his face, put on eyeliner, eye shadow, and mascara, his face progressively relaxing each time he moved on to another cosmetic. Once satisfied with his makeup, he reached up and grabbed one of the short-haired wigs perched before him.

"Joe!" Jonathan called out.

"Yeah?" Joe questioned as he pulled his wig over his head.

"What do you do for a living anyway?"

"You want the honest answer or the lie?"

"The honest answer."

"I don't have a job. I'm living off savings and unemployment checks."

Jonathan guffawed. "I'm jobless too—got fired last Friday!"

His wig in place, Joe started adjusting the bangs. "Why's that?"

"Why did I get fired?" Jonathan questioned.

"Yeah," Joe confirmed.

"I beat a corpse with a baseball bat!"

Joe froze. "What did you just say?"

"…uh…when?"

"Just now, Jonathan, what did you say?"

103

"I backed a truck into my boss's Fiat."

Joe smiled at himself, took a breath, and started adjusting his bangs again. "Cars can always get fixed."

"Not this one," Jonathan commented. "I banged it up pretty good."

Comfortable with his new look, Joe shifted in his chair so that he faced his bedroom door. He slipped on his heels and stood up. "Jonathan," he called out nervously.

"Yeah?" Jonathan replied.

"I'm about to come out."

"…okay."

"I've changed."

"Your clothes," Jonathan said. "I remember."

Joe walked over to his bedroom door and opened it.

Jonathan was sitting on the couch eating Ben & Jerry's Chubby Hubby ice cream out of the container with a spoon. He stopped eating and looked up. "You're dressed like a woman."

Joe smiled nervously. "Yep."

Jonathan's eyes were glazed and he looked slightly confused. "You're a cross-dresser?"

Joe nodded. "I am."

Jonathan cocked his head to the side. "Are you gay?"

"No," Joe replied calmly. "I just like dressing up."

Jonathan shrugged his shoulders and resumed eating ice cream.

Joe brought his arms out to his sides and spun around. "You're cool with this?"

Jonathan looked up. "It'll take some getting used to," he said with a mass of ice cream in his mouth, "but yeah, I'm cool with it."

Joe's smile grew. "Wow, thanks."

"I live in San Francisco," Jonathan commented. "It's really not that big a deal."

Joe clapped his hands together and started toward the kitchen. "Brunch!"

"Scrambled eggs and bacon," Jonathan called out as he scraped the bottom of the ice cream container. "If you have salsa, could you—" Jonathan broke off suddenly.

"Could I what?" Joe asked from the kitchen.

Jonathan didn't reply.

Joe walked into the living room and looked at Jonathan.

Jonathan was staring across the living room toward the TV.

"What?" Joe asked.

"You know…" Jonathan said slowly.

"Yeah?"

"…you look a lot like your ex-wife right now."

Joe glanced at the photo of his ex-wife and then looked back at Jonathan. "So?"

Jonathan looked at Joe. "Your wig looks like her hair. Your makeup…and the suit…Wow, man."

Joe sighed. "It's the same suit."

Jonathan pointed at the photo. "You're wearing that suit?"

Joe crossed his arms. "I kept it after the divorce."

"Why?"

Joe uncrossed his arms, walked over to the spot on the couch next to Jonathan, and sat down. "Because I bought it, and I liked it."

"And now you wear it."

"Yes."

Jonathan paused. "I'm confused."

Joe took a breath. "After Valerie and I graduated from college, I picked up a job as a technical writer for a company in Eugene. She picked up a sales job with Fisher Communications."

"Fisher what?"

"Fisher Communications. It's a media company based out of Seattle. They own a bunch of radio and television stations."

"Ah…"

"Anyway, her job kept her away from home. One week she'd be in Seattle, the next Portland, and the next some other place."

"Uh-huh?"

Joe looked off at the photo of his ex-wife. "I missed her and wanted to feel closer to her. So, I started bringing her nightgowns to bed with me, to lie next to them while I slept." He sat back and paused. "Soon I started wrapping the nightgowns around pillows and embracing them. Then, one night, after Valerie had been away for nearly three weeks, I put one of them on." Joe looked off wistfully and smiled. "The silk felt wonderful against my skin, and I slept more peacefully than I had in months. From that point on, I wore Valerie's nightgowns to bed whenever she was away." He looked back at Jonathan. "Before I knew it, I was dressing up in her clothes on a regular basis. Then—" Joe's voice faded.

"Then what?" Jonathan asked.

"Then one day, she arrived home early from work and found me sitting in the living room watching TV."

"So?"

Joe sighed. "I was wearing one of her skirts and a babydoll tee."

"What did you say to her?"

"The truth—that I missed her. That I wore her clothes to feel closer to her when she was away."

"How did she react?"

"She freaked out, told her parents, and left. Then a couple of months later, she filed for divorce." Joe dropped his head and stared off at the floor.

Jonathan sighed. "I'm so sorry."

Joe shrugged his shoulders. "What do you do?" he said dismissively.

Jonathan paused. "Why do you still dress up? I mean, if the relationship's over, what's the point?"

Joe looked at Jonathan. "It makes me feel good, more centered and at ease."

"Centered and at ease," Jonathan repeated. "I wish I had something that helped me feel that way."

Joe cracked a mischievous smile. "Ever try dressing up?"

Jonathan shook his head and smiled. "Not my thing."

Joe kicked off his heels, faced Jonathan, and pulled his feet up onto the couch. "Come on...Think of it as make-believe."

Jonathan's smile grew. "Don't even try, Joe. It's not gonna happen."

Joe smiled. "All right, I'll back off."

"Besides, I've never been much for make-believe."

"Since when?"

Jonathan huffed. "Since *ever*."

Joe smiled. "When you were a kid, you were all about make-believe!"

Jonathan shot a sarcastic thumbs-up toward Joe. "Right."

"Seriously. Everywhere we went, you insisted we save a space for your imaginary friend—" Joe paused. "What was his name?"

Jonathan smiled. "I think I called him *Joe's full of shit*."

"I'm serious," Joe insisted. "His name was..." He trailed off in thought. "Joshua!" he exclaimed. "His name was Joshua!"

The expression on Jonathan's face flattened. "Stop kidding around, Joe."

Joe paused and looked at Jonathan intently. "You don't remember Joshua?"

Jonathan huffed, stood up, and walked away. "I don't remember him because he never existed!" he exclaimed, raising his voice. He stopped short of the kitchen, turned around, and faced Joe. "You're fucking with me because I'm high!"

"I'm not fucking with you, Jonathan. When we were kids, you talked about Joshua all the time. You said he protected you."

Jonathan's body stiffened. He reached up and absently scratched his neck.

"Are you okay?" Joe asked.

"I'm fine!" Jonathan snapped back. He dropped his hand to his side and locked eyes with Joe. "Who did I say Joshua protected me from?"

"People," Joe said and then paused. "People who wanted to hurt you."

Jonathan narrowed his eyes and flared his nostrils. His face turned red. "Who did I say wanted to hurt me?"

Joe thought for a moment. "I don't remember."

Jonathan walked up to the couch and sat back down across from Joe. "Think, Joe!" he exclaimed. "Who wanted to hurt me?"

"I don't know," Joe pleaded. "You never mentioned a specific person. You just said *people.*" Joe looked away.

"Look at me," Jonathan said in a stern voice, staring intently at Joe.

Joe looked back at Jonathan. "Stop it, Jonathan. You're scaring me!"

Jonathan's eyes remained fixed on Joe. "Did I ever talk about a man named Robert Ray Lewis?"

Joe started to tear up. "Stop looking at me like that Jonathan. Stop it!"

"Did I?" Jonathan yelled. "I need to know!"

Joe got up, walked over to the front door of his apartment and opened it wide. "Get out!" he said as he wiped the palms of his hands over his eyes, smearing mascara across his temples.

Jonathan didn't move.

Joe reached up and pulled the wig off his head. "Leave, Jonathan!"

Jonathan took a deep breath, stood up, walked outside, turned around, and faced Joe. "I might have called him Bobby Ray," he said in a tense, but calmer voice.

Joe slammed the door and locked it. He held his breath and looked through the peephole.

Jonathan looked both ways and then stepped toward the door, raising his fist as if to knock.

Joe gasped, stepped back, and waited. He heard nothing. A moment later, he looked through the peephole again.

Jonathan was gone.

the emo poet

Standing a mere five feet four inches tall, fourteen-year-old Toby Paterson would be missed by most if it weren't for her thick, horn-rimmed glasses and habit of wearing her favorite bright green sundress far too often. Decked out in her usual best, she spent her summer days handing out poems to strangers and friends alike in front of The Beanery, a popular coffeehouse in Ashland, Oregon.

"Hey lady," a man said as he approached Toby.

Toby was holding a stack of blue index cards. She held one out toward the man. "Poem?"

The man paused, took the card, scanned it, and then handed it back. "I've already read this one."

Toby shuffled through her stack. "How about this one?" she asked, holding out another card.

The man took hold of the second card and looked it over. "I've read this one, too," he said as he handed it back. "Toby, I'm pretty sure I've read all of your poems." He walked up to the front door of The Beanery, pulled it open and looked back. "When you write something new, let me know."

Toby smiled. "I will. Enjoy your coffee."

"Thanks," the man replied with a smile.

Toby heard footsteps behind her. She turned around and saw the best-looking guy she'd seen in months. He was slightly disheveled and dressed in black. His eyes were sleepy and he was looking at a pocket watch.

"What time is it?" Toby asked.

"Excuse me?" the guy said, looking down at Toby, stuffing the watch into his pocket.

Toby pointed toward the pocket. "What time is it?"

"Two-fifteen," he replied and then pointed toward The Beanery. "They sell coffee in there?"

"And tea," Toby said with a smile.

"Thanks."

As the guy started toward the front door of The Beanery, Toby held out a card. "Poem?"

He brushed Toby's hand aside and kept walking. "I'm not religious, thanks."

"It's a poem."

The guy stopped, faced Toby, and took hold of the card.

"I write them down and give them to people to read."

The guy was silent as he looked at the poem.

Enamored by his face, Toby stood by watching intently. She admired his lips and his eyes before realizing that he was actually reading her work. "You're reading," she said at the same moment she wished she hadn't.

"Yes," the guy said in a near whisper, his eyes fixed on the card.

Toby knew the poem well. It was one of her favorites and so she mentally reviewed it as he continued to read.

In a room, a boy is laughing.
In the darkness, he is dancing.
With a cotton-filled bear
he got for his birthday.
He knew he should be sleeping,
but he just received it yesterday.

There was a knock on the door.
Then his mother screamed out angrily.
"God damn it, little baby!
What the fuck are you trying to do to me?"

Oh God it happened again.
Another boy destroyed from within.
No blood, no burns, no bodies bruised.
Words were the only weapons used.

When the guy looked up from the poem, he looked as if he was about to cry. "You wrote this?"

"I did," Toby replied sheepishly. "Do you like it?"

The guy smiled. "I love it."

Toby pigeon-toed her feet and blushed. "I've never had anyone react to one of my poems like that."

"What can I say," the guy said. "You caught me at the right time." He held up the card. "Can I keep this?"

"Of course," Toby said. "Yes."

"Thanks." He turned and started walking toward the front door of The Beanery.

"What's your name?" Toby called out.

"Jonathan," the guy said as he gripped the handle of The Beanery's front door.

Toby smiled. "Thanks for reading."

Jonathan smiled. "Thanks for writing poetry."

Toby stood outside for ten minutes before a sudden wind blew through and gave her a good chill. "Brrr," she said as she rubbed her hands on her forearms. She looked up toward the front door of The Beanery. "Lemongrass tea would do me good!" she said under her breath as she walked up to the door, pulled it open, and went inside.

The Beanery was a spacious rectangular building with massive windows and wood-paneled walls. The room had twelve or so tables and a countertop to the left of the front door. To the right of the front door, past the indoor tables, was an outside patio.

Inside The Beanery, Toby saw Jonathan sitting at a table. She smiled his way, but he didn't look up from his drink. After getting in line and purchasing a glass of lemongrass tea, she walked over to Jonathan, stood silently, and waited.

Jonathan looked up.

"Can I sit with you?" Toby asked as she pulled out the chair across from Jonathan and sat down. She set her glass on the table.

"Do I have a choice?" Jonathan questioned.

Toby wrapped her hands around her glass. "No."

Jonathan shook his head. "Shouldn't you be in school or something?"

"It's summertime," Toby said. "School doesn't start 'till the end of the month."

Jonathan took a sip of his drink.

"Are you a student at SOU?" Toby asked.

"I'm just passing through."

"Most people passing through get their drinks to go."

Jonathan looked out the window. "Before I can move on, I've got some thinking to do." He looked back at Toby. "Where're your poems?"

"In my pocket," Toby said as she let go of her glass of tea. "Wanna see another?"

"No, thanks," Jonathan said. He reached into his breast pocket and pulled out the card Toby had given him. "I want to ask you a question about this one."

Toby blew on her tea, steaming up her glasses. "What about it?"

"Is it about you?"

Toby didn't look up. "It's about my brother."

"So you were never verbally abused?"

"Just my brother." Toby took a sip of her tea. "I was the quiet one."

Jonathan held up the card. "Are all your poems this tragic?"

"For the most part, yeah."

"How do people respond?"

"You cried."

Jonathan stuffed the card back into his breast pocket and sat back in his chair. "I teared up; there's a difference."

"You cried," Toby repeated and then took another sip of her tea.

Jonathan looked away. "Yeah, well…"

"You said you had thinking to do. Thinking about what?"

Jonathan looked back at Toby. "The past four days of my life have been," he paused, "challenging."

"So you're thinking about life?"

Jonathan leaned forward and finished off his drink. "You could say that."

"I think about life a lot."

"Oh, yeah?"

"Yeah."

"Has it gotten you anywhere?"

Toby took a breath. "Well...I used to hope and pray for a better life, and now I'm starting to build one."

"What difference does it make," Jonathan said dismissively.

"The first brought me closer to God, and the other brings me closer to the life I want."

Jonathan paused. "You're a bright girl."

Toby smiled. "Thanks."

"What's your name?"

"Toby."

"Toby, what would you say if I asked your opinion on my life?"

"What would I say?"

"Yeah."

Toby smiled. "Uh...Yes! I mean, no one's ever asked me my opinion before, especially about something as important as their life."

Jonathan leaned forward in his seat. "What if the information you had to base your opinion on was whacked."

"Whacked?" Toby questioned.

Jonathan sat up. "Messed up. Troubled. Uneasy."

Toby's eyes widened with excitement. "Disturbed?"

Jonathan paused. "Yeah, disturbed."

Toby leaned forwarding her seat. "I would be totally and completely interested in anything that could be described as disturbed," she whispered. "Fire away."

Jonathan set the palms of his hands on the table, sat back, then leaned forward again. "Up until last Friday, I was a mortuary driver. Which pretty much means I picked up dead people and drove them to the mortuary I worked at." He paused.

"I'm with you," Toby said.

"Okay, so, last Friday, I picked up a guy named Robert Ray Lewis. There was nothing overtly strange about the pickup; it was just another dead body stuffed into the back of the hearse on yet another day of work. At least, that's the last thing I remember thinking before things got hazy." Jonathan stopped talking and looked out the window.

Toby paused. "Is that it?"

"No," Jonathan said, "I'm trying to figure out a way to say what I want to say."

"Just say it," Toby insisted.

Jonathan took a breath and looked back at Toby. "So things got hazy, and when I came to again, I'd beaten Robert Ray Lewis's body with a baseball bat." Jonathan pursed his lips and paused.

"*That's* it?"

"There's more..."

"Hold on a moment," Toby said as she picked up her cup of tea, took a sip, and then set it down again. "Okay, go on."

"I was fired."

"As well you should have been," Toby said nonchalantly.

"Yeah, and from that day forward, I've had a recurring dream I can't shake from my head." Jonathan looked down at the table. "I'm in a room. There's a large window to my left and a cracked-open door to my right. I'm planning to do something—but I can't remember what. I hear someone call my name. Then, I take a deep breath, close my eyes, and start to float. When I open my eyes again, I'm standing in the sky, holding purple lilacs in my hand."

"That's a cool dream," Toby said.

Jonathan locked eyes with Toby. "There's more to it than just the visuals."

Toby took a breath.

Jonathan looked down at Toby's cup of tea. "While I'm dreaming, I can feel Robert Ray Lewis's presence around me; I can feel his breath and the weight of his body pressing against me." He paused. "Are you sure you're okay with this?"

"Yes…Go on!"

"Above and beyond all this, friends tell me I've been talking in my sleep. That I cry out for Bobby Ray to leave me alone, to go away." Jonathan looked out the window. "And, I have a powerful feeling he molested me once, but I can't remember when. I also feel like I have family in Washington, but I don't know why." He looked back at Toby. "So here I am, scared, confused, and talking to you."

A moment of silence fell over the table.

Finally, Toby spoke. "You want my opinion?"

"Yes."

"Go north."

Jonathan blinked. "Go north?"

"That's all I got," Toby said, fiddling with her cup. "I don't know much about you, but I get the sense you need to touch base with that family you think you have."

"Why?"

Toby looked up at Jonathan. "Because it's the only thing you told me that isn't whacked."

Jonathan started to smile and then laughed.

Toby smiled. "Why are you laughing?"

Jonathan's laugh shifted to a chuckle. "Because you're right." He pressed his chair away from the table and stood up.

"Where are you going?"

Jonathan smiled. "North."

As Jonathan started walking toward the front door of The Beanery, Toby pulled a pen and a green card out of her pocket. "Jonathan!" she called out.

"Yeah?"

Toby wrote on the card, shielding it from Jonathan's view with her other hand. When she was done writing, she folded the card over and handed it to Jonathan. "When all of your questions are answered, read this card."

"Is it a poem?" Jonathan asked.

"No," Toby replied.

Jonathan slid the folded card into his back pocket and smiled. "Okay... When all my questions are answered, I'll read the card." He started back toward the front door.

"Can I write a poem about this?" Toby asked.

Jonathan looked back. "If you'd like to, sure, go ahead."

"Good," Toby said with a smile. "I know just the person to give it to!"

the joyful man

Just east of Eugene, Oregon is its sister city, Springfield. Bridging the two cities is Eastgate Woodlands Park, a triangular greenway along which the Willamette River flows. Within Eastgate, there's a six-foot-long bench that overlooks the river and provides a comfortable seat for Clark Gilmore—a joyful man.

Successful, with a loving wife and child, Clark lived in Eugene but traveled to the bench every Wednesday evening. There he sat, waiting for the sun to set, reflecting on life and the thanks he has for the gifts he's been given.

"Can I sit here?" a young man asked pointing to the end of the bench opposite Clark.

"Be my guest," Clark said.

The young man sat down, slouched, stuffed his hands into his pockets, and sighed.

Two minutes passed.

"I love the sound a river makes when it's traveling fast," Clark commented, as he stared off at the Willamette.

The young man glanced at Clark. "It's nice."

"And then some," Clark said, "My name's Clark."

"Jonathan," the young man replied with a nod.

"What brings you to the bench, Jonathan?"

"This bench?"

"Yes."

"I'm somewhere between heading home and continuing forward on a road trip I'm on. I pulled off the freeway to think things over."

"Amazing, isn't she?"

Jonathan paused. "Excuse me?"

Clark pointed. "The river."

A beat of silence passed.

"Uh, yeah, *she's* nice,"

"Do you have kids?"

Jonathan chuckled and shook his head. "No."

"Kids are gifts."

Jonathan glanced at Clark. "I'll have to take your word on that."

Clark turned and looked at Jonathan. "Last week, my little girl and I were walking down the street hand and hand, when all of a sudden she stopped, laid down on her belly, and stuck her ear up to the flower of a dandelion. She said she was listening to the flower. Looked up and asked me if I'd listen to it with her."

"What'd you do?"

"I got down on the ground and listened with her."

"What'd you hear?"

"I heard the joy of lying on the ground listening to a flower beside my daughter."

"You *heard* that?"

Clark nodded thoughtfully. "I did." He pointed his index finger up into the air. "Hold on a moment," he said as he reached into his back pocket for his wallet. From the wallet, he pulled out a posed picture of his wife, his daughter, and himself. He offered it to Jonathan.

Jonathan took hold of the picture and looked at it.

"That's my wife," Clark said with a smile. "Her name's Julie, and that's my daughter, June. She'll be three this November."

Jonathan handed the picture back. "You have a beautiful family."

"Thanks," Clark said as he took hold of the picture and tucked it back into his wallet. He started to cry.

Jonathan paused.

Tears continued to slip from Clark's eyes.

"Did something happen to them?"

Clark smiled, reached back and tucked his wallet away. "No, no...They're both fine—safe and sound at home. I just cry when I think about them—can't help it. The joy they bring me is so great, it's overwhelming." He stopped crying, reached up, and dabbed the tears from his eyes with the cuff of his shirt. "My wife and I are coming up on our fourth wedding anniversary."

Jonathan smiled uncomfortably. "Congratulations."

Clark took a breath. "She's a great woman."

"How'd you two meet?"

Clark smiled. "I hired her as an illustrator for a book I was working on—she's an artist. We started dating and married a short time later."

"What was the book?"

Clark smiled. "*The Cuddle Sutra*. Just like the Karma Sutra only it's about skillful cuddling instead of sex."

Jonathan nodded. "Clever."

"Thanks. This past month, it was translated into its fourth language."

"Good for you."

"Thus far, it's sold over three million copies worldwide."

Jonathan sighed. "That's great, really. I'm happy for you." He stood up and stretched his arms out above his head. "I should be getting back on the road." He dropped his arms back to his sides. "It was nice meeting you," he said with a wave. "Take care."

"If you leave now, you're gonna miss the sunset."

"It's cool," Jonathan said as he started walking away. "I'm not much for sunsets."

"Watching a sunset would do you good," Clark called out as Jonathan continued to walk away, "help pull you out of that pall your under."

Jonathan stopped walking, turned around, and faced Clark. "What 'pall'?"

"There's an air of death about you. Reminds me of myself, seven years ago."

Jonathan huffed. "Not to be rude, on account you seem like a nice enough guy. But don't presume for a second you're anything like me." Jonathan took a breath. "Because let me tell you, you're not!"

"How so?"

"How so what?" Jonathan questioned as he crossed his arms.

"How am I not like you?"

Jonathan glanced off at the river and then looked back at Clark. "Put simply, your life's blessed, and mine...mine's not!"

"My life wasn't always blessed."

"What?" Jonathan snapped back sarcastically. "Your book was once only a regional best seller?"

"No," Clark said calmly as he reached back and pulled out his wallet again.

"Thanks," Jonathan said as Clark pulled out a picture, "I've already seen your family."

"Not this family." Clark held the picture up toward Jonathan.

Jonathan uncrossed his arms, walked over, and looked at the picture.

It was wrinkled and worn, similar to the other picture only older. There was a different woman and a different little girl in it.

"Who are they?" Jonathan asked.

"My first wife and child."

Jonathan stepped back. "So you've been divorced, get in line."

Clark set the picture down on the bench, between the split of his thighs, and looked down at it. "They died in a plane crash, back in 1992—USAir Flight 405. They were taking off from New York on their way to Cleveland—careened into Flushing Bay during takeoff. The authorities said the crash was due to icing and pilot error, but I still felt guilty for their death. The guilt sat with me for two years, nearly tearing me apart, before Julie came along and showed me the way back."

Jonathan paused. "The way back to where?"

Clark looked at Jonathan and smiled, tears slipping from his eyes. "Joy."

Jonathan took a breath.

"I've felt sorrow and regret, beaten and worn. I've felt anguish, and I can see that anguish in your eyes."

Jonathan started to tear up. "What do you know about me?"

"Only what I see."

Jonathan glanced off at the river for a moment, sniffled, and then turned and walked away.

"If you hang in there," Clark called out, "there'll be joy for you, too!"

Jonathan didn't respond or look back, he just kept walking.

Clark took a breath and looked back at the river before him. He sat on the bench until the sun went down. After that, he stood up and left for home.

the chiromancer

Robyn Van Sant was born with the ability to perceive beyond the senses. This awareness was first realized when, as a little girl, she began to kiss her father's belly whenever he lay down. Only three years old at the time, when asked why she did this, she'd reply, "Your leaf is broken."

A couple of months after Robyn's kisses began, a dull pain started to creep into her father's back. Concerned, he went to his doctor for a checkup. At first his doctor dismissed the back pain as the product of overexertion. But then, Robyn's father made an offhand comment about the location of his daughter's kisses, and her seemingly non sequitur reason for giving them.

"She said your leaf is broken?" the doctor questioned.

"Yeah," Robyn's father confirmed as he buttoned up his shirt. "Cute, isn't it?"

"The pancreas sits in that same location, behind the stomach. It's about six inches long and...it's shaped like a leaf."

Robyn's father stopped buttoning his shirt and smiled uncomfortably. "You don't say."

The doctor continued, "Some pancreatic cancers don't produce symptoms until they've grown around nearby nerves. Such a growth could result in back pain similar to yours. So, if you don't mind, I'd like to run a few tests."

Two weeks later, Robyn's father was formally diagnosed with pancreatic cancer. Luckily for him, it was caught at an early stage, contributing to its rapid control and removal from his body. Still, were it not for Robyn's kisses, her father's nearly asymptomatic form of cancer would have, more than likely, resulted in his death—a sobering thought that drove Robyn's father to foster and encourage his daughter's gift.

Over time, Robyn began supplementing her clairvoyant intuition with insights gained through the ancient art of chiromancy, or palmistry. This coupling of techniques broadened her awareness of disease beyond physical sources to include spiritual sources as well.

Now thirty-six, Robyn lived and worked in Portland, Oregon, where she performed professional readings at a small boutique and bookstore called The Healing Space. She shared her standard 11 a.m. to 4 p.m. shift with Maggie, her close friend.

"Hump day begins!" Robyn exclaimed as she unlocked the front door of The Healing Space from the inside.

"I'd settle for a hump," Maggie commented from behind the service counter. "I've given up on getting laid."

Robyn turned around, smiled, and shook her head. "Maggie, I can't believe you sometimes."

Maggie sighed. "Believe it...I haven't been laid in months!"

Robyn walked up to the front of the service counter and gave Maggie a look. "That *isn't* what I was talking about."

Maggie shrugged her shoulders. "I'm sorry. I'm just frustrated."

Robyn reached out and gripped Maggie's hand sympathetically. "I know."

The Healing Space was a large square shop with vaulted ceilings. Hung high on the walls were Southeast Asian and African masks, tapestries depicting various Hindu gods and goddesses, and North, Meso-, and South American reproductions. Along the lower walls were shelves stacked with books about earth magic, faith healing, meditation, and related topics. The center of the shop was filled with a maze of tables covered in hand-carved animals, statues of Buddhist icons, ornate boxes, and incense trays. To the right of the front door was the service counter.

As Robyn let go of Maggie's hand, Maggie smiled. "Did you just breathe me in?"

"Why do you ask?"

"Because, I suddenly feel better."

"That's all you," Robyn said with a smile that flattened as she looked off toward the front door. She narrowed her eyes and grimaced.

"Something wrong?" Maggie asked.

"Someone very broken is coming this way."

"Who?"

The front door to The Healing Space opened and a young man walked in. He looked scruffy, his hair was tousled, and his eyes were swollen and red. "You do readings here?" he asked as he approached the service counter.

"We do," Maggie replied as she flashed a glance at Robyn, "But our reader isn't in right now."

Robyn looked at Maggie. "She's in."

"Are you sure?" Maggie whispered under her breath.

"I am," Robyn replied as she faced the young man, reached out, and opened her arms toward him. "This way," she said as she gestured for him to follow her.

He followed.

After a few steps walking backward, Robyn turned her back to the young man, continuing on toward the back of the shop. There, tucked into a recess, was a booth.

The booth was covered by a thick red curtain with gold tassels dangling off its hem. Robyn pulled back the curtain, revealing two cushioned seats separated by a small wooden table. A wall sconce illuminated the interior of the booth with a soft light. After gesturing for the young man to sit, Robyn sat down across from him, pulling the curtain closed behind her. "What brings you here?" she asked.

"I need to know what's wrong with me."

Robyn clasped her fingers together and rested her elbows on the table. "I can help you with that. But I'd like to relax you first…Is that okay?"

The young man took a breath. "I suppose so."

"What's your name?"

"Jonathan."

Robyn smiled a soft and pleasant smile. "My name's Robyn."

"Hi, Robyn."

Robyn's smile grew. "Hi, Jonathan." She unclasped her hands and reached across the table. "Give me your hands."

Jonathan reached out and clasped Robyn's hands.

Robyn closed her eyes. "Now, Jonathan…"

"Yes?"

"Close your eyes." Robyn felt a rush of energy pour out of Jonathan and into her hands. She took a breath and the energy spiraled up her arms, into her shoulders, down her back, and settled in her belly. She exhaled and the energy rose up into her chest and out with her breath. She continued cycling breaths until the energy spouting from Jonathan's hands settled into a steady stream that fluttered like a ribbon in the wind. Robyn felt Jonathan go limp. When she opened her eyes, she saw him leaning against the inside wall of the booth. His eyes were closed, his breathing was shallow, and he looked liked he was asleep. She let go of his hands, brought her hands up to her mouth, cupped them, and then blew into the space created. As she blew, she opened her fingers toward Jonathan, her breath filling the air around him.

Jonathan's eyes opened. He slowly sat upright, a dazed look on his face. "I passed out…"

"You did," Robyn replied calmly.

"I didn't see that coming," Jonathan said as he wiped his hands over his face.

"How do you feel?"

Jonathan blinked, then smiled. "Good…Really, good."

"You're carrying a spirit inside you," Robyn said bluntly.

Jonathan cocked an ear toward Robyn. "I'm sorry, what?"

Robyn ignored Jonathan's question. "Please, give me your dominant hand," she said as she reached both her hands out across the table. "The hand you write with."

Jonathan paused for a moment and then reached out his left hand, resting it palm side down.

"Palm up, please."

Jonathan flipped his hand over, letting it curl up at first, and then stretching it open wide. "You're gonna read my palm?"

"I am," Robyn replied. She grasped Jonathan's hand, holding his thumb and pinky finger apart.

"What do you see?"

Robyn paused. "Your hand suggests a life marked by traumatic experiences. You're a nervous person, prone to outburst and distrust. You're also an aesthetic, with spiritual sensibilities."

"What's an aesthetic?"

Robyn looked up. "Someone who's concerned with or appreciates beauty."

"You get that from the lines on my hand?"

Robyn looked back down. "I get that from the shape of your hand. You're lines tell me different things."

"Like what?"

"You're emotionally unstable and prone to depression."

"All true," Jonathan commented. "But, if you don't mind, could you elaborate on that comment you just made, the one about my 'carrying a spirit inside me.' What was that about?"

Robyn looked up. "Before I can help you understand that," she said in a soft voice, "I need to learn about you as a person. Your hands help me do that."

Jonathan paused. "Okay."

Robyn looked back down. She finished reading Jonathan's heart line, moved on to his head line, and then read his life line. After she was done, she looked up again. "Something catastrophic occurred in your life when you were young, something you were aware of but refused to accept."

Jonathan said nothing.

"Please, give me your other hand."

Jonathan pulled back his left hand and stretched out his right.

Robyn took his hand in hers and started to read. She was silent for nearly a minute.

"What does my right hand say?"

"Your left hand tells me who you are," Robyn said without looking up. "Your right hand tells me who you were." She looked up, took a breath, and pushed Jonathan's hand back toward him. "You've cycled before."

Jonathan swallowed. "What does that mean?"

"You're the reincarnate of another. Another whose spirit is now yours but who still holds on to a pain that precedes your life."

Jonathan huffed. "You're crazy."

"You know what I'm saying is true. You feel it. The sorrow, the inexplicable pain, it wells inside of you. You feel it, and it weighs you down."

Jonathan pulled his hands off the table and crossed his arms.

"The emotions—the ones rising up inside you right now, they block you from resolving your pain. They're why you can't see clearly, why the truth is blurry to you."

Jonathan started to tear up. "What else am I supposed to do, huh? I'm not a robot. I'm a human being. I'm gonna feel something—I can't help it!"

"Your feelings aren't the problem," Robyn said calmly. "Your lack of control over them is."

Jonathan sighed.

"At what age did you feel a shift in your life, a shift from before to now?"

Jonathan sniffled. "What are you talking about?"

"You know what I'm talking about. When?"

"I don't know."

"Try to remember."

"I told you," Jonathan said angrily, "I don't know!"

"You're lying, Jonathan," Robyn said matter-of-factly. "You know, but you're refusing to say."

Jonathan's nostrils flared. "Nine, okay? When I turned nine! I stopped feeling connected. I pushed away from my family, my friends, anyone who loved me. And," Jonathan started to cry. "I still do it today."

"Don't cry, Jonathan," Robyn said in a pacifying tone as she held her hands out across the table. "Not now. Give me your hands."

Jonathan unfolded his arms, wiped his eyes, and extended his hands toward Robyn.

Robyn took hold of Jonathan's hands, breathing in deeply and exhaling slowly, cycling his sorrow out of him, though her, and away.

Jonathan's shoulders sank and his face softened.

Robyn let go of Jonathan's hands. "It's only a temporary fix, but I need you clear and unemotional for a few moments more."

Jonathan took a breath. "Okay," he said calmly.

"Something happened to you this morning, something that's happened before, but until now your emotions have blocked you from seeing it clearly. What was it?"

Jonathan swallowed. "I had my recurring dream…Only it was different this time."

"Describe it to me, just as it happened today."

Jonathan looked off toward the closed curtain. "I was standing in the middle of a room. Like before, there was a large window to my left, only this time I looked out it and saw a street sign."

"What did the street sign say?"

Jonathan looked at Robyn. "Mercer Way."

Robyn smiled. "Good...Tell me more."

"To my right was a door that I'd cracked open."

"Why'd you crack it open?"

"So they could see I was serious." Jonathan reached up and absently started scratching his neck with his right hand.

"Serious about what, Jonathan?"

"Serious about what I was going to do." Jonathan paused.

"What were you going to do?"

Jonathan shuddered. He lifted both his hands to his neck and started scratching, a terrified look on his face.

"Tell me, Joshua!" Robyn exclaimed. "What were you going to do?"

Jonathan stopped scratching, dropped his hands onto the table, closed his eyes, and took a labored breath. "I was going to pretend to hang myself."

"But, you did hang yourself, Joshua. You did."

Jonathan opened his eyes. "I didn't," he said calmly. "I only wanted them to think I was going to."

"Who did you want to think that?

"Mom and Dad."

"But you're not with us anymore. If you didn't do it, why aren't you here with me now?"

"Because..." Jonathan started to tear up, again.

"Because what?" Robyn question sternly. "Spit it out!"

"Because...Bobby Ray found me first." Jonathan started sobbing. "He walked in and saw me standing on the chair with the rope around my neck and held my ankle while he read the note I left for Mom and Dad. When he finished reading he pulled my leg down and kicked the chair out from under me." Jonathan gasped. "Bobby Ray killed me! Not me! Bobby Ray!" He erupted into tears as he continued to cry, "Bobby Ray killed me, Bobby ray killed me…" fading into a whimper as he dropped his face into his hands.

Robyn allowed Jonathan time to feel his pain.

Gradually, Jonathan's tears subsided.

"Jonathan."

"Yeah?" Jonathan replied as he wiped his tears off his face.

"Do you remember what you said?"

Jonathan sniffled. "Yeah…"

"Do you remember what I called you?"

Jonathan locked eyes with Robyn. "You called me Joshua."

"Do you know why?"

Jonathan took a breath. "I do."

Robyn leaned forward in her seat. "That's it for us. The rest is up to you. Control your emotions and a path to relief will present itself. Give in to your emotions, and you'll have to deal with your pain throughout this life and into the next."

"What we just did didn't make things right?"

Robyn took a breath. "The spirit inside you isn't resting, Jonathan. I can still feel it stirring."

"Help me get rid of it!"

"I can't Jonathan. I can only help you help yourself."

Jonathan started to whimper. "What am I supposed to do?

"Keep searching, keep learning…The closer you get to the truth, the more you'll know you're on the right path—the path to relief."

Jonathan dropped his head and dug the palms of his hands into his eyes. "I'm so tired," he cried. "I don't know if I can take anymore."

Robyn reached out and gripped Jonathan's hands, pulling them back down to the table.

The skin around Jonathan's eyes was beet red.

"You can do it," she said encouragingly as she held Jonathan's hands. "You hear me? You're almost there. Keep pressing on, keep learning..."

Jonathan's shoulders relaxed. "I suppose I could start looking for streets named Mercer Way."

"I know where Mercer Way is," A voice said. The red curtain suddenly slid open.

Robyn and Jonathan flinched in surprise, and then looked up at Maggie, who stood with a smile and a folded sheet of paper.

Robyn's face flushed pink with anger. "You were listening in on my reading!"

Maggie blinked. "I was worried about you."

Robyn stepped out of the booth and shot Maggie a look of disappointment. "That doesn't give you the right."

Maggie shrugged her shoulders. "Sorry."

Robyn snatched the folded sheet of paper out of Maggie's hand. "What's this?" she asked through a sigh as she looked it over.

"It's a map of Washington State," Maggie said.

Robyn looked at Jonathan. "Does Washington mean anything to you?"

"It does," Jonathan replied as he slowly climbed out of the booth and stood up.

Robyn walked over to the service counter, opened the map, and spread it out.

Maggie walked over and pointed at a road that snaked around the perimeter of Mercer Island—a small island city outside Seattle. "Right here," she said with a satisfied grin. "Mercer Way!"

Jonathan walked over and looked down at the map. "She's right," he said as he glanced at Robyn. "That's it."

"Then that's your destination," Robyn said.

Jonathan grabbed the edge of the map. "Mind if I keep this?"

"It's yours," Maggie said.

"Thanks," Jonathan said as he took hold of the map, folded it up, and stuffed it into his back pocket.

"Do you have any idea what you'll find on Mercer Island?" Robyn asked Jonathan.

"Pretty much, yeah," Jonathan said as he pulled out his wallet.

Robyn paused. "It's on the house."

Maggie rolled her eyes and looked away.

"Are you sure?" Jonathan questioned.

"I am," Robyn replied in a soft voice.

Jonathan smiled. "Thank you so much," he said as he reached out and hugged Robyn.

"You're welcome," Robyn replied, hugging Jonathan back. "Be safe and remember, the closer you get to the truth, the more you'll know you're on the right path."

"I will," Jonathan affirmed as he stepped back. He started toward the front door of the shop. "Thanks again for the map!"

"No problem," Maggie called out as the door shut behind Jonathan. She looked at Robyn. "How are you?"

"Tired," Robyn said as she looked off toward the front door. "That's one troubled kid."

"Aren't we all?" Maggie commented.

"Not like that…"

Maggie paused.

"I'm gonna go get some coffee," Robyn said, breaking the subtle but noticeable tension between her and Maggie. "Do you want any?"

"I'm good, thanks."

Robyn reached behind the counter, picked up her purse and then walked over to the front door. Before opening it, she paused and looked back at Maggie. "Say, Maggie."

"Yeah?" Maggie questioned as she situated herself behind the service counter.

"You're gonna get laid this weekend."

Maggie smiled. "I knew you were breathing me in!"

the forgotten

Reginald Lewis, a retired mechanic, and his wife, Maxine, lived a quiet, unassuming life in a modest three-bedroom home in Mercer Island, Washington. By all external appearances, their lives were conventional ones. They smiled kindly to others at the local grocery store. They regularly attended community events and fundraisers. They were good neighbors, keeping a well-ordered and clean home, inside and out. Still, belying Reginald and Maxine's outward appearances was a secret. A secret they had buried, along with their first and only child, Joshua, back in April 1974.

Joshua Lewis was a lively nine-year-old boy who was well liked by all who knew him. But his grades had been progressively slipping, and his teacher, Mrs. Gainsbrook, was concerned. If things didn't improve, he'd have to repeat his fourth-grade year. Reginald and Maxine were equally concerned by their son's drop in grades but were at a loss for what to do about it.

Reginald owned and operated a successful automotive repair shop in downtown Seattle, and Maxine was his office secretary and accountant. Their days and early nights were booked solid six days a week, and Sunday, their only day off, provided little time to devote to Joshua and his scholastic struggles. Frustrated, Reginald worked out a deal with his brother, Bobby Ray, to step in and help.

An unemployed truck driver, Bobby Ray hadn't had a regular source of income for nearly six months. Broke and without options, he asked Reginald for a job at the garage. Reginald said no, claiming he couldn't afford another employee, instead offering another option.

"Here's what I *can* do for you," Reginald told his brother over the phone. "You can stay at my home while you're looking for a job. I won't charge you rent and I'll keep you fed."

"Why would'ya do that?" Bobby Ray asked suspiciously.

"So you can watch over Joshua while we're working. His grades have been slipping and we're starting to fear he might have to repeat the fourth grade. If you were around, urging him to stay focused and study, Maxine and I would be mighty thankful and consider your effort payment for room and board. What do you say?"

"When can I move in?"

In early January 1974, Bobby Ray moved into Reginald and Maxine's house. Over the course of the months that followed, Bobby Ray lorded over Joshua every weekday evening and Saturday day. Although Reginald and Maxine were pleased with that fact, Joshua was not. In protest, he started staying late at school, not coming home until he knew his parents where there. And, when Ms. Gainsbrook started insisting he go home, even going so far as to take him home herself on occasion, he began telling lies. All this, Reginald believed, Joshua did in an effort to get out of having to study.

By April of 1974, things looked dire. Four months into Bobby Ray's move, the end of the school year was fast approaching, and Joshua's grades still hadn't improved. Unless Joshua pulled a one-eighty in effort, he would repeat the fourth grade. Adding to this already troubling situation was the fact that Bobby Ray, Joshua's study supervisor, had picked up a part time trucking job that kept him away from the house on weekends—leaving yet another loophole for Joshua to study less. Everything came to a head late one Sunday afternoon, April 21.

Reginald and Maxine were away on their routine trip to the grocery store, and Joshua, having insisted he wanted to stay home and study, was left alone at the house. When Reginald and Maxine returned, they found Bobby Ray sitting in the living room watching TV.

"What are you doing here?" Reginald asked as he walked into the house, holding a bag of groceries. "I thought you weren't gonna be back until tomorrow."

"I double-timed my drive so I could get back a day early," Bobby Ray replied coolly.

"Where's Joshua?"

"In his room, I suppose. I haven't checked."

Reginald walked into the kitchen and set his bag of groceries down on the counter. "Joshua!" he called out. "Come help your mother and me with the groceries."

Joshua didn't reply.

A couple of minutes later, after Reginald, Maxine, and Bobby Ray had finished bringing the groceries in from the car, Reginald called out for Joshua again.

And, again, Joshua didn't reply.

Frustrated by her son's lack of response, Maxine walked to the back of the house and up to the door to Joshua's room. It was closed. "Joshua," she called out sternly. "Come out here right now!" After pausing for a moment, she angrily gripped the doorknob to Joshua's room and swung the door open. There in the middle of the room she saw her son dangling at the end of a makeshift noose tied to his ceiling fan.

While Maxine screamed and wailed, Reginald and Bobby Ray cut Joshua's body down. Ten minutes later, the paramedics were on the scene, but it was too late. Joshua was dead.

The authorities believed foul play was involved. But after their investigation revealed that Joshua had gathered the rope, tied the noose, and set the chair beneath him, there was nothing more for them to pursue. They closed the case and filed it as a suicide.

With no note left behind or any indication from Joshua as to why he might do what he apparently did, Reginald and Maxine were left to grieve—and for twenty-five years, never fully understand the details of their son's death.

The doorbell rang.

Reginald looked over the Puget Sound Energy bill he was holding, peering out through the space above his reading glasses. "Are you expecting someone?" he asked Maxine.

Maxine was sitting at the kitchen table across from Reginald. She set her needlepoint down and shot him a look. "If I was expecting someone, you'd be the first to know about it."

The doorbell rang again.

Reginald sighed and stripped off his reading glasses, setting them and the bill down on the table. As he started toward the front door, he reached his hand into his left front pocket, pulled out his pocket watch, and looked at the time—it was 5:30 pm.

"It's probably just a solicitor," Maxine called out.

"It better not be," Reginald grumbled. "We put up a sign."

The doorbell rang a third time.

Reginald pulled the front door open.

A young man was standing on the porch outside. His clothes were clean, his hair was combed conservatively to the side, and his face looked freshly shaven.

"If you're selling something," Reginald said as he pointed at a small metal sign above the doorbell, "we don't welcome solicitations."

"I'm not selling anything," the young man said.

"Then, what do you want?"

"Is your last name Lewis?"

"Yes," Reginald replied hesitantly.

"Did you have a son named Joshua?"

"Excuse me?"

"Did you have a—"

"I heard what you said," Reginald interjected. "Why are you asking?"

"I know things about him. Things you'll want to know."

Reginald's nostrils flared. "I don't know what game you're trying to play, but I'd advise you get the hell out of here before I call the police!"

Maxine walked up behind Reginald and gently placed a hand on one of his shoulders. "What is it? What does he want?"

"Nothing," Reginald snapped back as he glared at the young man. "He was just about to leave." He slammed the front door shut.

"I know things about Joshua!" The young man called out from behind the closed door. "Things about his death, reasons why." He paused. "Bobby Ray's involvement!"

Maxine looked at Reginald. "Open the door."

Reginald looked back at Maxine defiantly. "No."

The young man continued. "There's a coffee shop called Bauhaus Books & Coffee. It's on the corner of Melrose and Pine in Seattle. I'll be there all night. Please come, talk to me—I know things about Joshua. Things you'll want to know!"

Maxine gripped the doorknob. "Step aside, then."

Reginald turned and pressed his back against the door.

"What's going on, Reginald?"

"Can't you see? He's trying to scam us!"

Maxine stepped back, crossed her arms and gave Reginald a hard look. "Reginald Lewis, step away from that door, now!"

Reginald stepped away from the door.

Maxine stepped forward, gripped the doorknob, and swung the front door open.

The young man was gone.

"Hello?" Maxine called out, her voice cracking.

There was no reply.

Maxine shut the door, walked into the kitchen, and started anxiously pacing back and forth.

Reginald walked in behind her. "Baby, you don't think he was telling the truth, do you?"

Maxine stopped pacing and looked at Reginald. "Why'd you block the door?"

"He's a scam artist, Maxine, trying to play on our emotions."

"How do you know that? Huh? How?"

Reginald was silent.

Maxine left the kitchen, entered the bedroom and closed the door behind her.

Reginald shook his head, sat back down at the kitchen table and went back to looking over his bills.

Five minutes later, Maxine stormed out of the bedroom and started walking toward the front door.

"Where are you going?" Reginald asked from his seat at the kitchen table.

"For a walk, Reginald!" Maxine opened a closet near the front door. She pulled out a double-breasted camel hair coat. "I need to clear my head."

"Do you want me to go with you?"

"No," Maxine said as she slid her coat on and buttoned it up. "I want to go alone."

"You're not…"

"What?" Maxine snapped. "I'm not what?"

Reginald glanced at his car keys dangling off a hook near the kitchen phone. "Nothing."

"I'll be right back," Maxine said as she walked out the front door.

A few moments later, Reginald thought he heard the sound of the garage door opening. He paused and listened, but heard nothing more. So he dismissed the sound as a figment of his imagination. But then, a moment later, he heard the sound of his Lincoln Continental start up. Erupting to his feet, he rushed toward the front of the house just in time to see Maxine driving away.

Bauhaus Books & Coffee marked the gateway to the Capital Hill neighborhood of Seattle. Lining its walls were bookshelves crammed with used books. Huge floor-to-ceiling windows provided views of passersby, the Space Needle, and the distant Olympic Mountains beyond. The ambiance was cozy, providing refuge for college students, struggling artists, and the like. If one preferred a quiet place to contemplate life, people watch, or study, Bauhaus's upstairs tables obliged. If, on the other hand, one wanted to be seen or easily found, Bauhaus's bottom floor was the place to sit.

Having taken advantage of the magnetic hide-a-key that Reginald kept underneath a wheel well of the Lincoln, Maxine drove out to Capital Hill in search of the young man. She found him in Bauhaus Books & Coffee, just where he said he'd be, sitting at a bottom floor table, hunched over a glass of coffee. She walked up, pulled out the chair across from him, and sat down, unbuttoning her coat. "You have ten minutes," she said as the young man looked up at her.

The young man quickly sat upright in his chair. "Thank you for coming," he said hurriedly.

Maxine could see he was nervous.

"Would you like something to drink, a muffin, or something?" the young man stammered. "I just had a Top Pot donut, they're delicious." He gestured toward to the service counter. "I could get you one."

Maxine finished unbuttoning her coat and crossed her arms. "Nine minutes," she said with a cold look on her face.

"I understand… My name's Jonathan and I know things about your son, Joshua. Things I think you should know."

Maxine was silent.

"While you and your husband were away, Joshua was looked after by Bobby Ray, correct?"

"I'm not here to provide information," Maxine said. "I'm here to hear what you say you know about the death of my son." She stood up. "If you don't know anything, I'm going home."

"No, no, no…" Jonathan said pleadingly, as he gestured for Maxine to sit back down. "I'm sorry… Please, stay. I'll get to the point."

Maxine took a breath and sat back down.

Jonathan continued. "When you and your husband were away, Joshua was left alone with Bobby Ray. When this happened, Bobby Ray molested him."

Maxine took a deep breath.

"Joshua was terrified of Bobby Ray and so, for a time, he said nothing. Then one day he mustered up the strength to tell his dad, your husband, what was going on. But your husband didn't believe him.

"Joshua was desperate to be believed, so he decided to stage a suicide attempt. He thought that you and your husband would discover him and realize he was telling the truth about Bobby Ray. That he was serious about what was happening."

Maxine started to tear up.

"Are you okay with this? I don't have to be so blunt."

Maxine wiped the tears from her eyes. "Continue."

Jonathan took a breath. "Joshua staged the suicide in his bedroom. He stepped up onto a chair, tied a rope off his ceiling fan, and looped the other end around his neck. He left a note for you and your husband to find."

Maxine sniffled. "There wasn't a note."

Jonathan pursed his lips. "There was, but Bobby Ray discovered Joshua before you. He held Joshua's leg while he read it, and then pulled his leg out and kicked the chair out from beneath him when he was done."

"You're saying Bobby Ray killed my son?"

Jonathan started to tear up. "For fear of his brother, your husband, discovering he was a child molester—yes."

Maxine paused. "Did Bobby Ray tell you this?"

"No."

"Then how do you know these things?"

"I can't say…You wouldn't believe me." Jonathan looked up over Maxine's head and his eyes widened. "Joshua wrote a draft of his note—"

"Get up Maxine, we're going home!"

Maxine turned around and saw Reginald. He was furious. "Sit down and listen to the boy."

Reginald gritted his teeth and pointed at Jonathan. "If you go anywhere near my wife or me again," he screamed, "I swear I'll fucking kill you! You hear me? I'll fucking kill you!"

Jonathan slid out of his seat and stepped back, keeping the table between himself and Reginald. "I'm not looking for trouble, sir. I'm trying to help you and your wife learn the truth about your son's death."

Reginald raised a fist toward Jonathan.

Maxine stood up. "That's enough, Reginald!"

Reginald put a hand on the small of Maxine's back and started walking her toward the front door.

"Joshua folded up his note and buried it at the bottom of a can of nails!" Jonathan called out as Reginald and Maxine reached the front door. "A coffee can filled with nails!"

Reginald and Maxine left.

On the way home from the coffee shop, Reginald grumbled, "Do you know how embarrassing it was for me to ask Bob Lenore for a ride to Seattle?

Maxine sat silently in the passenger's seat of the Lincoln, an angry look on her face.

"*Where's your car, Reginald?* My wife snuck off in it to talk to a con artist!"

Back at home, Reginald parked the Lincoln in the driveway, got out, and pulled open the garage door.

Maxine got out of the car, walked past Reginald, and started looking around the garage. "Do we have a coffee can full of nails?"

"I can't believe you're taking that guy seriously. He's a liar Maxine, looking to scam us out of money!"

Maxine started pulling open the trays of a hip high toolbox. "Do we have a can of nails?" she screamed.

"We don't!" Reginald snapped back.

Maxine paused and gave Reginald a hard look. "Did Joshua tell you Bobby Ray molested him?"

Reginald was silent.

"Answer me, Reginald! Did Joshua tell you!"

"Yes!" Reginald exclaimed. "Yes…"

Maxine's anger rose near the point of hysterical rage. "And you never thought to tell me?"

"You knew, as well as I did—Joshua wanted to get out of his studies. He'd say anything…"

Maxine took a breath. "Even after we found our son dead, you never questioned that he might have been telling you the truth? That Bobby Ray might have done what Joshua said he had?"

Reginald paused. "Bobby Ray's my brother."

"Joshua was our son!" Maxine exploded into tears. "Do we have a coffee can filled with nails?"

Reginald's shoulders sank. He walked over to an old dresser pressed against the wall, knelt down onto his knees, and opened the bottom drawer. He pulled out a coffee can filled with rusted nails. "There's nothing but nails in it."

Maxine wiped the tears off her checks and then crossed her arms. "Dump it out."

Reginald turned over the can of nails—a folded piece of paper fell out.

Maxine reached out an open hand toward Reginald. "Give it to me."

Reginald handed Maxine the piece of paper.

Maxine unfolded it, saw Joshua's handwriting, and started to read:

> *Dear Mom and Dad,*
>
> *I'm sorry. I don't want to upset you. But Bobby Ray touches me when you are away. He tells you we study together, but he lies. I told Dad what he does, but Dad said I was a liar. But, I'm not a liar.*
>
> *Mrs. Gainsbrook taught us a song. I forgot who sang it first, but it's called Bird Song. My favorite part is the one that goes,*
>
> *If you hear that same sweet song again, will you know why? Anyone who sings a tune so sweet is passing by.*
>
> *Laugh in the sunshine, sing, cry in the dark, fly through the night.*

Sometimes I sing that song and wish, I could fly away.

Maxine and Reginald were stunned, their minds scrolling through pain, sorrow, regret, and anger.

Maxine looked at Reginald. "Where's Bobby Ray?"

Reginald took a deep breath. "I don't know."

"You don't know, or you won't tell me?"

"I don't know...He lived in Everett with Mom, until she died. After that, he moved to California. But it's been nearly fifteen years. He never called, never wrote. I lost contact. You know that."

Maxine folded Joshua's note back up and walked into the house. Inside the kitchen she walked up to the phone, picked it up and dialed 411.

"City and state, please."

"Seattle, Washington."

"What listing?"

"Bauhaus Books & Coffee."

"Have a nice day."

Maxine heard a computer-generated voice state the phone number for Bauhaus. She waited on the line until she was patched through.

"Bauhaus Books & Coffee," a male voice said.

"Hello, my name's Maxine Lewis."

"Yes?"

"Is there a young white man with brown hair, wearing a black shirt and slacks sitting at a table in the center of the room?"

"There was, but he got in some kind of argument with an older couple and left a while ago."

"Could he have simply moved to another seat, or maybe be out front?"

155

"I saw him leave. He didn't look like he was going to stick around." There was a pause. "People were starting to stare."

"Thanks," Maxine said as she hung up.

"Is he still there?" Reginald asked.

"No."

The phone rang.

Maxine paused.

"Maybe they found him," Reginald said.

Maxine glared at Reginald, "How could they call me back?" she said as she reached for the phone.

"Caller ID," Reginald commented.

"Hello," Maxine said into the phone.

"Is there a Reginald Lewis, there?" a woman's voice asked.

"Yes, hold on please." Maxine held the phone out to Reginald. "It's for you."

"For me?" Reginald questioned as he took hold of the phone. "Who is it?"

"A woman," Maxine commented as she walked away and sat down at the kitchen table.

"Yes," Reginald said into the phone.

"My name's Donna Wright, the girlfriend of your brother Robert." She paused.

Reginald looked at Maxine. "Yes?"

"I came across your number while going through his belongings." The woman paused. "He passed away last week. He had cancer."

Reginald swallowed. "Where are you calling from?"

"Oakland, California."

Reginald took a breath.

"His wake was earlier this week; he was buried in Hayward at the Lone Tree Cemetery. I'm sorry you had to find this out after the burial, but I had no idea he had a brother, or family for that matter. He never mentioned either. If you want, I can send you the key to his apartment, and you can go through his things."

"How long were you two together?"

Donna paused. "Twelve years."

"Keep his things, consider them yours."

"Do you want my number, in case you change your mind?"

"That won't be necessary," Reginald said. "Good-bye." He hung up the phone and looked at Maxine.

"What is it?"

"Bobby Ray's dead."

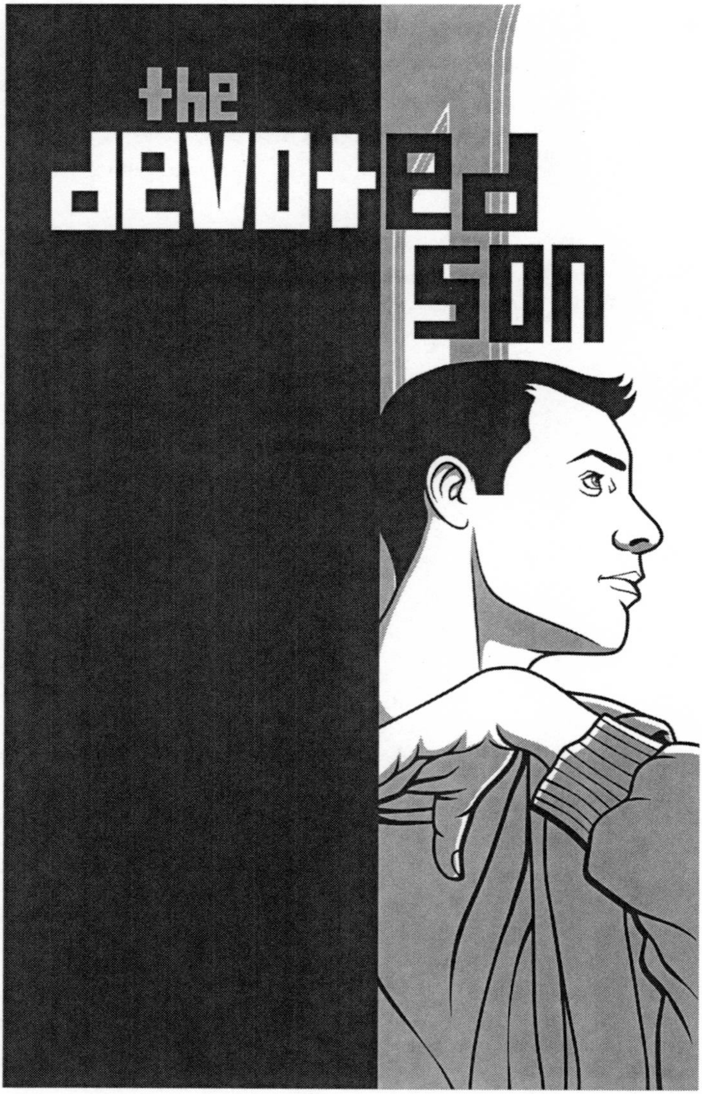
the
devoted
son

the devoted son

Russell Avery left Vancouver on a Greyhound bus headed for Seattle. His ultimate destination was Arcata, California, but to get there, he had to transfer to another bus at the Seattle terminal.

Upon his arrival in Seattle, Russell confirmed the transfer with his new driver and stowed his luggage. He tucked himself into a seat at the back of the bus, settled in, and fell asleep. When he awoke, he turned to his right and saw a middle-aged man sitting next to him.

The man was eating from a bag of Doritos, humming "mm-mm" in between each bite.

Russell looked at the man and sighed.

"Where're you going?" the man asked, his breath reeking of processed cheese.

Russell grimaced. "Arcata."

"Damn it," the man said as he looked toward the front of the bus. "I didn't realize we were heading down the 101."

"We're not," Russell said, "at least not directly. I'm getting off in Redding. A friend's picking me up and driving me to Arcata from there."

"Thank goodness!" The man looked down, pulled out another chip, and stuffed it into his mouth. "I'm heading to Sacramento," he said while chewing.

Russell stood up. "Could you pull your legs in for a sec? I need to use the restroom."

"Sure."

The bathroom was in line with Russell's row. He pulled the door's latch but it didn't budge.

"Occupied!" a man's voice called out from within.

"Sorry about that," Russell said as he scanned the rest of the bus. There were two rows of paired seats, all of which were taken, except for one. The empty seat was along the isle, adjacent to a man who was turned and looking out the window. The man's messy brown hair and face seemed familiar to Russell, so he stepped closer for a better look. As he continued down the isle toward the familiar man, he started to smile. When he reached the empty seat, he sat down. "Jonathan?"

Jonathan turned away from the window. "Yes?"

Russell reached out a hand for a shake. "I'm not sure if you remember me—my name's Russell."

Jonathan reached out and shook Russell's hand, smiling tentatively.

"We met at Martin's house earlier this week."

Jonathan's face brightened up. "Yes, of course, Russell. How are you?"

"Good," Russell said.

Jonathan paused for a moment. "If I remember correctly, you were heading up to a town in Canada?"

"Harrison Lake, just outside of Hope. To dispense my father's ashes."

Jonathan pursed his lips, "That's right...I forgot, I'm sorry."

"Please, don't be," Russell insisted. "It was a beautiful thing. I was only supposed to stay a day, spread my father's ashes, and head back home. But then I started checking out the area, visiting places he'd talked about. Before I knew it, I'd stayed all week. It was like my father was with me the whole time, sharing stories and showing me places he'd loved."

Jonathan smiled. "I'm glad...Didn't you fly, though?"

"I flew up," Russell said. "But I only had enough money for a one-way ticket." He sighed. "So I'm bussing it home." He thought for a moment. "Don't you have a car?"

Jonathan's smile grew. "It's a funny thing about that car. I held it together with patches and glue for a good part of the last five years. And, for a while, I started thinking there was nothing that could stop it. But then, just as I was about to leave Seattle, on my way back home, my radiator failed. The car overheated and the engine seized."

"Where's the car now?"

"On the side of the road in Seattle."

"Are you going back for it?"

Jonathan smiled. "Nah...It's staying there."

"Wow," Russell commented.

Jonathan shrugged his shoulders. "It got me where I needed to go, so I'm okay with it."

"Where was that?"

Jonathan took a breath. "Mercer Island."

Russell smiled. "So you found what you were looking for?"

Jonathan nodded slowly. "I did...Yeah."

Russell noticed an ease in Jonathan's disposition, one he hadn't the first time they'd met. He cocked his head to one side, interested. "How do you feel now?"

"Alive," Jonathan said, taking a deep breath. "Like a weight's been lifted off my shoulders. Like I'm breathing for the first time." He paused. "I feel amazing. And...It's gonna take some getting used to."

Russell sat back, smiled and nodded. "I get that."

Jonathan smiled. "Do you?"

Russell chuckled. "I do."

Someone to Russell's left coughed loudly.

"You're sitting in my seat," a man said.

Russell looked up at the man. "Sorry, about that. I was visiting a friend." He looked back to Jonathan.

Jonathan was looking away, pulling a folded green card out of his back pocket.

"Take care, Jonathan." Russell said as he stepped aside, giving the man back his seat.

"Yeah," Jonathan replied, focused intently on the folded green card. "Nice talking to you..."

Russell started toward his seat. A couple of rows back, he stopped. He was curious how a simple card could distract Jonathan's attention like it did, so he turned back and looked over Jonathan's shoulder.

Jonathan was holding the card open. He had a massive smile on his face. Written in black pen across the card were the words:

Congratulations...You did it!

Breinigsville, PA USA
06 May 2010
237450BV00001B/1/P